Natural Tendencies

Natural Tendencies

Joan Mellen

The Dial Press
New York

Published by
The Dial Press
1 Dag Hammarskjold Plaza
New York, New York 10017

First printing
Designed by Ann Gold

Library of Congress Cataloging in Publication Data
Mellen, Joan.   Natural tendencies.
I. Title.
PS3563.E4427N3   813'.54   80-22066
ISBN 0-8037-6576-2

For Francine Toll

In the gardens of certain Buddhist temples there are trees which have been famous for centuries—trees trained and clipped into extraordinary shapes. Some have the form of dragons; others have the form of pagodas, ships, umbrellas. Supposing that one of these trees were abandoned to its natural tendencies, it would eventually lose the queer shape imposed upon it; but the outline would not be altered for a considerable time, as the new leafage would at first unfold only in the direction of least resistance. . . .

—Lafcadio Hearn
Japan: An Interpretation

. . . he saw once again, as he had felt them close beside him, Odette's pallid complexion, her too thin cheeks, her drawn features, her tired eyes. . . . and with that old, intermittent fatuity, which reappeared in him now that he was no longer unhappy, and lowered, at the same time, the average level of his morality, he cried out in his heart: "To think that I have wasted years of my life, that I have longed for death, that the greatest love that I have ever known has been for a woman who did not please me, who was not in my style!"

—Marcel Proust
Swann's Way

Part
One

Chapter One

*F*rom the debilitating heat, the corrosive steam, of the Kyoto August, Judith Frank sought shelter in Kaji's Antique Emporium on tiny Shinmonzen Street.

Inside the shop it was cool. Ivory porcelain objects about a century old shone softly in the semidarkness. They were scattered about at random with a disdain for what, to elegant, noncommittal Kaji and his parchment-skinned assistants, must have seemed the shiny vulgarity of their too recent vintage.

But to Judith, Kaji's was a treasure house, a wonderfully easy access to arts ancient and remote. She lingered over the porcelains, marveling that these artifacts could have attained the present without so much as a crack or a blemish.

On a narrowly elongated, shallow platter of mysterious utility, with the patina of an aged eggshell, were painted three laughing, cavorting clowns with mouths wide open and eyes tightly shut in merriment. Fan-shaped, fluted dishes depicted gay scenes of everyday life: geisha lifted their kimonos so that they might bathe their feet in an ice-blue river while a half-naked man perched on a rock onshore pointed in derision—or in affirmation of all the teeming life before him. Chubby, round bowls unex-

pectedly contained a little hump at the bottom, a fat pro-
trusion where one would expect a hollowed-out place. On
one, a crowd of drunken revelers in defiantly elaborate
costumes wove their way across its surface. Their faces
contorted in abandon, without the remotest concern for
public opinion, they reflected a greedy energy to tear at
and mock the world they had newly mastered.

These porcelains of the last century were painted in
the brightest of colors, ranging from persimmon and tan-
gerine to jade green, peacock blue, and midnight purple.
Their gray borders gave way to silver, bronze outlines to
gold. Elated birds and flowers opened to capacity surrounded the human figures in motion, their billowing gar-
ments lifted into the air by the invisible winds of time and
change they celebrated with so much exuberance.

Judith could afford to purchase only one. She chose a
large, round bowl. Within a musician dressed in an orange
kimono embossed with a shower of tiny gold-leaf blossoms, his jet-black hair glossy, thick, and luxurious, sat on
a silver cushion playing a samisen, his eyes half-closed in
concentration, his body undulating to an internal rhythm.
He seemed totally unaware of three listeners standing behind him, arms and legs moving in harmony as they
swayed to the music. Hypnotized, they had been cast beneath a spell that afforded them such transcendence they
had no desire to be disenchanted. Beguiled by the musician's strange, unearthly sounds, they had discovered their
own best selves. Their kimonos were merely pale gray,
their features less sharply defined than his. For they, after
all, moved in a realm of less grace, less refinement of texture. If it were not for him, they would not exist.

Framing the musician, as the bottom of the bowl met
the concave enclosure of its walls, was an elaborately

draped purple curtain embroidered with a thousand cherry blossoms and held apart by an orange ribbon which must have been cut from the musician's kimono. There he sat upon the raised bottom of the bowl as if it were a stage. Who could doubt that he was at one with his world, wholly sufficient unto himself, distant, inaccessible, forever to be admired as both subject and object of the work of art.

She had wandered from one shop to another, leafed through stacks of woodblock prints from which wild-eyed Kabuki actors glared up at her, traced her finger around the china faces of old samurai dolls in faded robes, admired tall standing screens on which were painted in gold leaf ancient battles pursued with unrelenting intensity by single-mindedly undeviating warrior clans, only there at last to have captured—him.

Judith had occasioned a great deal of interest on quiet Shinmonzen Street. From within darkened, seemingly unoccupied shops she was the object of long stares, frank and unfurtive since it was entirely appropriate to scrutinize a presence so out of keeping with order and decorum.

On this street, really no more than an alley, it was as if she had emerged upon a platform where bright lights pointed up every detail of her person.

What the gentlemen of Shinmonzen Street saw was the entity "foreign woman," a species whose size lacked delicacy and proportion. By Japanese standards she was somewhat too large, too broad-shouldered. Her features, recalling the peasant stock of her Russian-Jewish forebears, were too primitive, too crude to be of any appeal here. Fine discriminations were not to be awarded to foreigners. Worse, she was most immodestly attired in a bright orange, green, and black nylon print dress (the kind travelers packed along with boxes of Woolite). The flamboyant colors of that dress blinded those staring eyes, outraged them. Such colors were acceptable only for the ingenue, never for a woman more than twenty. A woman so indelicate could not be seen as a woman at all.

The crash diet Judith had embarked upon after receiving the invitation to come to Japan from the *Nichinichi* newspaper had helped to bring her back to how she had looked on the day four years earlier when her last lover had told her he was no good for her and departed for San Francisco, his conscience clear. Even before that she had never believed she was pretty; at least the kind of men who appealed to her would never think her so. And if her ideas were somewhat unorthodox, the men she had most admired and yearned for were profoundly conservative. Once she had met such men at fraternity houses where, coldly self-confident, holding themselves back as if they were pearls of great price, they had appraised her, a Jewish girl from The Bronx, according to measurements she could never hope to meet. Now in their forties, sleek and prosperous, such men could be spotted in expensive restaurants with elegant blond wives, hard and self-assured in their mink coats and lacquered hairdos, women too muted to express need, women who, like themselves and the Japanese, knew, at whatever cost, how to keep up appearances.

She believed that if anyone could ever love her, it would have to be because she saw more deeply than other women, was more clever. She had published three books on film by the time the *Nichinichi* committee had pondered over her strange interpretation of the great film director Kuronuma, whom she saw as a democrat and even, for postwar Japan, a revolutionary. Tenure as a professor of

English literature at a university had given her the space to ponder such esoteric subject matter.

What pulled her into Japanese cinema was its sense that history was alive in the present, the easy continuity in which the Japanese could define themselves by who they had been as a nation. In the sixties she had felt as if she and her friends were alive within the history of their own time. But when the marching was over, and the energy of the sixties gave way to the increasingly vacuous, motionless nostalgia of the seventies, she turned to the excitement of a culture where history was kept alive in the hearts of the people as an entirely natural phenomenon, as in the films of Kuronuma. Frequenting darkened movie houses she could be comfortable in the role of spectator. In her work she had returned to the back seat she had always sought.

Since childhood she had been a model of diligence, the compulsive *A* student. It had begun as a defense to shield herself from the sadistic shouting of her father. She had known only the dark side of the Jewish family, stripped of both nurturing concern and neurotic demands for achieving children.

Hunched over her books, she had given herself up to doing what was required: arithmetic tables and spelling lists as a youngster, geometry and Spanish in high school, statistics and philosophy in college. She dazed herself into a paralyzing boredom.

She sat and she worked. It was what she knew. She became skillful at taming ideas, constructing labyrinths and then adroitly guiding the readers of her essays and books through to some newly coherent whole.

Raphael, her last "relationship," had been what she'd chosen him for being—yet another man incapable of sustaining intimacy, uncomfortable with the requirements of caring, unwilling to love. She had become determined four years ago never again to risk dissolving into dependency, the vulnerability of relations with men, the invariable rejection and the pain. She would not be swallowed up whole again, not so long as the mind could serve as an insulating fortress. She became so accustomed to repressing desire that it seemed entirely natural. She tried a series of therapists; they stirred up her pain like sediment at the bottom of a bottle of vintage wine. These encounters, neither shattering nor reorganizing the old patterns, became unbearable in themselves. She herself could not sustain them.

Then she began to call herself a recluse. She insisted that the only world that mattered was that of her work. Thoughts became more real than people. So what if her pleasures were all of the mind? They were unthreatening. And didn't they, too, possess an ardor of their own?

At the close of each day she felt pale and tired, depleted, while the pile of crisp, perfectly typed white pages grew. Each day she sat and gave herself up to those pages. Evenings, exhausted, she'd read or watch television. She rarely left her old-fashioned, roomy, Upper West Side apartment at night. She wasn't afraid of the perils of the streets, but of scattering her energy. She worried that she wouldn't be fresh for the coming day's work. Then a day when she wasn't teaching would be irretrievably lost and she would have to work all the harder.

Facing the world outside—students who would grow surly and rude upon discovering that they were required to write complete sentences, a recalcitrant editor demanding that one of her books be cut for financial reasons—always produced a jolt for which she was ill-prepared, left her off-balance. Agitation had not been banished completely. But the details of life were reduced to a minimum.

Her doubts about whether this was life enough grew more faint as time lengthened. But if loving ceased, the self remained untorn. And wasn't this liberation enough?

Months earlier, when she'd seen the photocopied form announcing the *Nichinichi* contest on the faculty bulletin board, she had removed it without hesitation. She'd folded it neatly into her briefcase and the next day mailed off to Tokyo her Kuronuma essays which had been written for one of those obscure film magazines amenable to articles about Japanese cinema. It was work. It was what she knew.

But when the call from Kimura, the New York correspondent for *Nichinichi*, had come notifying her that she had won and specifying the day she was to arrive in Japan (the *Nichinichi* never doubted that all its winners would accept), she had been terrified. Frantically she searched for an excuse to decline. She could find none. Enveloped by a sense of the unreality of this unlikely adventure, she had accepted.

As she left the shop with her newspaper-wrapped purchase, the stares of all those invisible eyes on Shinmonzen Street finally penetrated her consciousness. Feeling as if her flesh were now in serious danger of melting, tightly clutching her porcelain bowl for reassurance, for the certainty it gave her of the structured and hermetic beauty of Japan, she quickly walked to busy Sanjo Street and whispered "Miyako Hotel" to a taxi driver wearing immaculate white cotton gloves and a not inscrutable look of disdainful curiosity.

Chapter Two

*T*he tiny room in the Miyako Hotel was furnished in nondescript blond wood in imitation of the bland modernist furniture of fifties America. The bed was inelegantly covered with a polyester striped bedspread of red and green. The oversized bureau stood squarely in front of the narrow single bed while a wide window oversaw a gray view, overwhelmed by ugly, jerry-built low stucco dwellings. Judith couldn't help feeling the *Nichinichi* committee had contemptuously shunted her here out of the conviction that she wouldn't have appreciated a view of the true Kyoto with its shrines and temples anyway.

Time weighed heavily after she returned from Shinmonzen Street. The air conditioning did little to relieve the sense of suffocation that continued from street to hotel. She was overcome by the same feeling she experienced at home whenever for some reason she was not able to get to her desk in the morning and work. In two days she had already seen as many temples as any human being could. She decided not to do any more sightseeing. Tomorrow she would have to open a panel discussion with a speech about Japanese cinema, as the *Nichinichi* hosting committee had instructed her before her departure from Tokyo.

But no one had told her what time to be ready, just that it would be on Tuesday. But was it to be at one, or at four, or at eight? She didn't know. How she would have loved to decline this particular event! She should have said she didn't know enough, she really was familiar only with the films of Kuronuma and then not even with all of those. What had she to say about Japanese film in general?

But the *Nichinichi* had been insistent. There was no space in their determination for her to evade what was obviously a long conceived design. She could think of it only as an ordeal to be dreaded. Worst of all, it was to be televised throughout Japan in accord with that internationalist posture that had motivated the contest in the first place. The purpose of this panel discussion, which had been spoken of in hushed voices by the committee, was to make the *Nichinichi* cosmopolitan, open to the outside world, like its major rival, the more highly respected *Asahi Shimbun*.

She ate dinner in one of the hotel restaurants. No one spoke to her. The next morning she waited in her room, pacing, reading over her remarks with dissatisfaction, then casting the pages aside. At two she went down to the lobby, staring first at one face and then at another. Where was the *Nichinichi*? If she settled herself in one of the restaurants for lunch, they might arrive and depart for the panel discussion without her. She sat down in a chair in the lobby and waited some more.

By three o'clock no one had appeared. She checked the desk again; the surly clerk, making it clear he was at the limit of his patience, reported coldly that there were *still* no messages. She wondered if the meeting had been canceled. Its star attraction, the avant-garde film director Koshima, might have backed out at the last moment.

Only a few days earlier Judith had interviewed Koshima at one of the meetings which were part of her tour and indefatigably arranged by her main host, Mr. Shimizu, the *Nichinichi* film critic, who usually stayed the hour to provide moral support. But this time, having introduced her to Koshima, he had departed in uncharacteristic haste.

Elegantly attired in a three-piece white silk suit, the chubby Koshima, rather tall for a Japanese of his generation (he was in his mid-forties), didn't seem the angry young man of his reputation, but a pillar of prosperity, respectability, and finesse. He answered her first questions patiently, though without particular good will. Then, with no warning, he had become contemptuous, speaking disparagingly of Kuronuma as well as many other great names in Japanese filmmaking.

She had been thunderstruck. "But we admire Kuronuma very much in the West. It was his work which led to my interest in Japanese films."

"He has nothing to do with me," Koshima replied coldly.

Perplexed, she had persisted. "But don't you admire any of his films?"

"No."

Koshima then proceeded to give one-sentence replies to the remainder of her questions. When she asked about the image of women in his own films, he said that he had nothing to do with the "bluestocking movement" either.

And yet she hadn't been able to stop herself from returning to the subject of Kuronuma. "I could understand a young avant-garde filmmaker in the West regarding John Ford as old-fashioned. He would of course himself be searching for new cinematic forms. But that wouldn't warrant his dismissing Ford's work or ignoring his contribution to American cinema, would it?"

Koshima had fallen silent.

"Wasn't Ford as innovative for his time as many young directors are today? Don't we require a historical sense?" She felt proud of herself for allowing Koshima to save face by transferring the problem to an American example.

"I have no patience with foolish sentimentality," Koshima said at last. "Such sentimentality only serves as a pretext for resisting what one doesn't understand."

She gave it up. His tone had been so abrupt. Further dialogue had become impossible.

This time Koshima had no doubt canceled at the last minute. The hotel clerks, who stared boldly each time she relinquished or recaptured her room key, had simply forgotten to give her the message.

Certain that this must be the case, she went to the Chinese restaurant in the hotel basement and ordered shrimps with peanuts, chicken with ginger, and steaming white rice. She ate voraciously and quickly because if the newspaper people did come to the hotel to collect her (although by now it was clear that they had changed their minds), they surely wouldn't look for her here.

Returning to the lobby, she vaguely recognized two officious-looking men as members of the committee which had assembled on the second day of her arrival in Japan to greet her as one of the winners of the contest. But although she now stood no more than two feet away from them, they seemed not to see her at all. Yet who could they be looking for but her?

She approached one of them and asked, "Are you looking for me?" It was all she could muster.

The man stared squarely at her and replied, "Yes, it is late, we must leave."

Soon a cluster of people were in motion. Judith followed as they pushed their way through the revolving doors of the Miyako Hotel into a still steamy late afternoon.

Outside stood a man and his wife whom the newspaperman who had spoken to her briskly introduced as Mr. and Mrs. Saito. Their bows were perfunctory in a distant if correct way.

"We have also been staying at this hotel," said Mr. Saito, eying her with displeasure.

Murmuring her acknowledgment, Judith lapsed back into silence. Despite the weather, Mrs. Saito was dressed in a navy gabardine suit with a peplum jacket, as if only this costume could confer the authority suitable to her age and status as the wife of a prominent man. On the top of her head was perched a tiny white hat, its little veil pulled back. Clutching a large navy leather handbag much too big for her, she hovered close to her husband. Her pursed lips and the harsh little lines around her eyes left no doubt that, size notwithstanding, she was far from frail.

Crushed into the back seat of a taxi with the Saitos, Judith couldn't think of a thing to say. Mr. Saito's expression seemed determinedly vacant and impassive. For the entire forty minutes it took to reach the conference center, not a single word was spoken, in any language. She allowed her mind to go blank as she waited for the afternoon to be over.

The building before which their car drew up had once been considered as a possible home for the United Nations. Nestled neatly in front of a border of mountains on the periphery of Kyoto, it was monumental, with white columns in the fake Greek revival style and large bay windows along the façade. Adorning the roof were the flags of all the nations, as if the building were determined to retain its candidacy as the center for a world organization.

Before the debate, the panelists were gathered into a small anteroom to be served tiny cups of strong coffee. Mr. and Mrs. Saito stood side by side, talking with a journalist from the *Nichinichi*. Another panelist, a nondescript man named Kato, professor at a university, had already arrived. So had Koshima, dressed once more in his white silk suit. Koshima was engaged in conversation with a man who had settled into the role of avid listener. Judith stood by herself, expectant and apprehensive, waiting for something to happen. Still no one talked to her, but perhaps this was only because no one felt like struggling with English just before the proceedings were to begin. Then Mr. Saito approached her: "I wish to present you with these copies of my books," he said, holding out five volumes but not relinquishing them.

"Thank you very much," Judith replied abstractedly. She waited. Mr. Saito seemed at a loss about what to do next. Then one of the interpreters interrupted them, a bustling young woman in a sort of schoolgirl uniform.

"We would like to borrow your text for a few moments," she announced abruptly.

Judith tightly held on to the pages, unwilling to give them up. They were handwritten none too neatly. In an instant the fingers of the woman closed upon the manuscript and she disappeared from the room without another word. Judith murmured apologetically, "I had no idea anyone would be looking at them," to her retreating back.

A *Nichinichi* functionary announced that it was time to begin. The participants were led single file into the auditorium, where they were each placed behind a small desk facing the audience. A pair of earphones lay before them. On Judith's desk her manuscript had miraculously reappeared. She stared out at the audience wishing she were any place but here. She felt like a fly under a microscope. She couldn't see the simultaneous translators from her vantage point but she knew they were elevated somewhere above her. Could she trust their accuracy? Before her sat rows of students bussed in by the *Nichinichi* like so many cattle, settled into thickly upholstered seats each with its set of earphones. Most of them were barely twenty, but no longer carefree or young; they seemed like incipient businessmen—there was only a sprinkling of women in the group. As if by design they had all dressed like the woman who had taken her manuscript, in white shirts and dark blue or black ties or pale blue or pink blouses and navy-blue skirts. A sea of homogeneous forms, expressionless, waiting, they sat shoulder to shoulder with no seat unoccupied. A deadly silence reigned over the gigantic auditorium.

A short man with heavy-rimmed glasses so huge they seemed to weigh down his entire face strode onto the stage. Entirely at ease and in his element, he introduced himself as Mr. Harada, representative of the *Nichinichi* newspapers, this year celebrating their centenary with programs like this one held at cultural centers throughout Japan.

"We are very much interested in the problem of international communication and exchange," Harada proclaimed exuberantly. "What image of Japan and the Japanese lies in the minds of foreigners?"

Judith felt all eyes on her. It was she and not Japanese movies that was to be the subject of the day, she the foreigner who had been invited to Japan by the *Nichinichi* because the essays she had written about Kuronuma had seemed so strange to them. A week before, when she was introduced to the *Nichinichi* executives, the publisher had told her, as they sat in his penthouse office with its spectacular panoramic view of Tokyo, that she had been selected because they found her approach to the films of Kuronuma "peculiar." He drew out the word in English, savoring it. She had smiled and said nothing. She did not ask what it was about her ideas they found "peculiar." She shrank from knowing. The meeting ended with her being whisked to the sub-basement of the building where limousines waited to take her wherever she wished, to her hotel, to her next appointment, to the bottom of the sea of Japan. They were, they told her, "at her service."

Harada droned on. "Kyoto was once an important town for film production," he continued, "and as it occupies a great position in the arts of Japan, it is all the more significant that we are holding this panel discussion in the ancient capital of Kyoto."

Judith kept a fixed expression, attempting to emulate the rapt attention of the audience. Harada introduced the panelists. It seemed he was finally about to sit down. Then, instead, he added, "This Kyoto International Center is not conveniently located in terms of transportation. We have prepared two buses and will have a shuttle service at the conclusion of the meeting. Please pay attention to the panel discussion and enjoy the film which will follow without worrying about transportation problems."

The young people in the audience remained expressionless at this news that the logistics of their departure had been settled. Solicitude was taken for granted. Nor were there smiles of cynicism or embarrassment at

Harada's final words: "I hope the results of this panel discussion will give a depth of feeling to you in your hearts."

At the rear a foreigner suddenly entered the auditorium, a fair-haired man, his skin as white as if it had been bleached. Judith was sure it was Paul Meredith, the American specialist in Japanese movies who had lived in Tokyo for thirty years.

She had once attended a lecture he had given at Japan House in New York. She remembered being struck by his ageless quality; from a distance he could have been forty or fifty-five. After his talk, he had chatted patiently with eager Americans as he smoked cigarettes from a long lapis lazuli holder.

That was the winter Kuronuma had attempted suicide. Judith decided to ask Meredith why one of the greatest directors in the history of film had wanted to take his life. She had approached him with trepidation, noting as she got closer the deepening lines on his face and its asymmetrical oddity. Under his right eye there was a deep, sagging pouch, while the skin under the left was as smooth as that of a boy.

He inhaled and dared her to make sense. The right eye twitched. She had thirty seconds to declare herself.

"Is Kuronuma all right now?" she blurted out. "Why should so great an artist not want to live?" She knew she sounded like an adolescent. Weren't perceptive people more likely to despair and seek an end to the sufferings of this world? Wasn't this one of Kuronuma's great themes? She even knew there was a tradition among Japanese artists to take their own lives at the moment they felt their life's work to have been completed. Why was she acting like such a fool?

Meredith seemed to smile at her benevolently. His

violet blue cats' eyes looked as if they were backlighted. The right eye now stopped twitching. Would he be friendly and recognize how much they had in common, how much she admired his book about Kuronuma? Surely he must have been as upset about the suicide attempt as she.

"Everyone asks me about Kuronuma's suicide attempt," Meredith said. "It was a gory mess. According to the maid who found him, blood was splashed over everything, bathtub, shower, the tiles were submerged under an inch of sticky red blood. What I can't figure out is how he could slash himself so many times and still survive. The doctors found sixteen major cuts. He just stood in the shower bleeding away. Actually he recovered quite quickly. He obviously had no intention of killing himself at all."

He had seemed to take positive delight in this bloody anecdote, as if he were amused that Kuronuma had botched his suicide. Was he also implying that Kuronuma had botched his work too, that his films had been overrated and that he had tried to kill himself because he had *lost* his powers rather than because he had reached the height of his artistry? In any case, Kuronuma seemed a joke to him, and she was a joke as well, a foolish American.

She knew he must see her as no better than the pallid Japanophiles he had to put up with at such occasions, who deserved no better than to be treated to a lurid account of Kuronuma's folly. How could she let him know that she was different?

A tall, thin, expensively dressed woman with thinning brown hair and an enormous emerald ring had walked up and there was Paul Meredith calling out "Lily!"

kisses on both cheeks, raptures of remembered evenings with fashionable people. He turned away as if Judith were not still there. Then she had walked as quickly, as unobtrusively, as she could to the farthest corner of the room.

Now here he was, of all people the one least likely to offer any comfort, alien as these inscrutable Japanese. The terror of knowing that her introductory remarks were to come first was intensified by that Anglo-Saxon presence leaning against the rear wall of the auditorium, smoking a long cigarette through the same lapis lazuli holder, ready to judge her, ready to find her wanting.

She decided to talk about her unpleasant interview with Koshima the week before. It had weighed upon her mind all the time she was in Kyoto. What had she done to offend Koshima? She wouldn't use his name in her speech, but he would understand that she was speaking to him.

"I'm surprised at the hostility toward Kuronuma among young filmmakers here," she began. "And this disdain is not directed only toward Kuronuma. It seems to include all the old masters of the Japanese film. Even those who were considered innovative for their time. They shouldn't pose any threat to younger people creating new forms of their own."

Academically, in the manner with which she was most comfortable, she went on to describe a line linking old and young in the postwar film, all the while deliberately avoiding mentioning the name "Koshima." As she spoke she was intensely conscious of him, a few feet away, poker-faced in his white silk suit, so obviously the celebrity of the afternoon and still so hostile toward her. Was it because she had proven herself to be out of touch with

Japanese realities by having selected to write her essay about the obsolete Kuronuma? She was aware that she spoke before an audience too young to have seen Kuronuma's best films, which were rarely revived in a country where there were few art houses.

Resolutely she launched into further appreciation of the accomplishments of Kuronuma, as if in his rehabilitation lay some justification of herself as well.

"One of the reasons I began to write about films was that I loved the movies of Kuronuma so much," she concluded. She sat down relieved that the most trying part of the meeting must surely be over. She considered how she must appear to these assembled Japanese. She was the only woman on the platform, attired, Mrs. Saito's costume had made clear, in a manner entirely inappropriate. The bright pink nylon dress with its floral pattern may have packed well for a long voyage, but it was far too garish, too girlish for this occasion, and it made it too obvious that, even more inappropriately, she wore no restraining undergarments. Nor did a woman of thirty appear in public in Japan with long, unfettered hair. If she were of any interest to those assembled here, it must be a result of her strangeness. There was no applause, only so impersonal a silence that despite the staring faces she felt as if she had spoken to an empty hall. Casting a quick sidelong glance at Koshima, she observed his masklike face staring straight ahead. He seemed not to have written anything in preparation for his coming rebuttal on the pad provided on his little desk.

Professor Kato was now at the podium, a tall, thin man, his clothes hanging on his bones. His prominent hawklike nose pointed upward, framed by a thick head of uncombed, unruly black hair. "There were some concepts which were very difficult for me to grasp listening to Miss Frank," he began.

Judith wondered what concepts he meant since she wasn't aware of having introduced any.

"Humanity," "nature," "feudalism," intoned Kato, "these were the terms Miss Frank used, but I was not quite sure what she meant by these words. I don't know if what she said was clear to other people, but it was not to me. I could not understand these key words, so I don't know how to evaluate Miss Frank's presentation."

She had said that Kuronuma had been critical of the vestiges of feudalism in modern Japanese life. But she couldn't remember having invoked "humanity" and was positive she never mentioned "nature." Could the interpreters in their isolation chamber have mistranslated her remarks?

Meanwhile Kato waxed on, invoking the myth that the Japanese will forever be inscrutable to outsiders who cannot possibly illuminate matters of Japanese culture. Shared terms of reference did not exist. Judith sat in a daze as the very possibility of discussion was dismissed. For these Japanese intellectuals the cliché of saving face demanded that in an alien mode of discourse differences of opinion had to be proven nonexistent.

She saw all possibility of being convincing, of saying anything acceptable, slip away. Self-assertion in such a context would not only be futile, but ridiculous.

Kato finally launched into a condescending paean to Kuronuma. But since she had already traced an argument that depended upon taking Kuronuma's films seriously, Kato could not also do so.

Since Judith, a foreigner, had expressed admiration for Kuronuma, Kato must prove that Kuronuma had nothing to say to the Japanese, that the Japanese did not even understand what the conflict between good and evil in Kuronoma's films was about. Judith had described his skill at editing, his subtle use of the dissolve, and the traveling camera with which he entered the action of his films. "Kuronuma has exhausted himself with the traveling shot," Kato added smugly, delighted with his felicitous turn of phrase. Meanwhile, like the others, she sat motionless, as decorum decreed, without expression, her eyes blankly directed toward the audience.

Meredith still stood there, leaning against the rear wall of the auditorium. What must he be thinking about all this? What did he really feel about Kuronuma's films? When she had been invited to Japan, she had decided not to look him up. They could never be friends. She wasn't his type. After that first painful encounter at Japan House in New York she had tried to find out more about him, and everywhere she went she heard that he was manipulative, perverse, even twisted. You might think he was your friend and then he would betray you, but in such a devious way that he could never be called to account for it. Someone said his favorite sport was to play upon the weaknesses of his fellow Americans so that in this foreign land they became even more confused and disoriented than was necessary. Yet his visiting countrymen couldn't resist him. Everyone knew that Paul Meredith could be counted upon to initiate a visitor to Japan into Tokyo nightlife at its most raw and tawdry. Then he was both sympathetic and distant, consoling, advising, encouraging the timid to go forth. The people he seemed to favor were those willing to lose themselves in Japan, responding to this mysterious civilization by making themselves perpetually vulnerable and acquiescent in self-abasing subservience to whatever happened to them here.

Yet when she arrived, out of loneliness and the panic

of lacking a single acquaintance in Japan, she had called him up. Her heart had pounded in fear, but she had managed to dial his number. "Let's meet for a drink this afternoon," he proposed. He was affable, civilized, even friendly. She was surprised. The rumors about him must have been exaggerated. She told him that she would be coming with the *Nichinichi* film critic, Mr. Shimizu.

Then most of the allotted hour had been lost to a mix-up. She had sat with Mr. Shimizu waiting for Paul Meredith to appear in the Old Wing of the Imperial Hotel, as they had agreed. No sign of him. The hour was slipping away. Finally Mr. Shimizu went off and found Paul strolling about in a New Wing she had not known even existed. She suspected that only his knowledge that Mr. Shimizu would be present had ensured that he turn up at all. When she had asked him during the course of their conversation whether he could introduce her to Kuronuma, he had refused emphatically—they were no longer friends, Kuronuma "hated" him. His violet blue eyes refused to confirm or deny the truth of this. No, that was the one thing he could not do.

Until today that was the last she had seen of him. How unlucky (and yet, of course, how logical) that of all the American expatriates floating about Japan, he should be the one to turn up in the outskirts of Kyoto to watch her being patronized by these men who believed she had no right to voice any views whatever about anything Japanese.

Her speech, however hesitantly delivered, had described Kuronuma as a rebel against feudal norms, one of the first directors in Japan to dramatize the value of individual judgment. Kato, zealously mindful of distinguishing his views from those of the foreigner, now

insisted that Kuronuma at heart had always been a traditionalist, the main reason why his work had no contempo-
rary relevance. He referred to the final image in a
historical film made by Kuronuma in the fifties which Paul
Meredith had once written was the first Japanese film ever
made. In the film's concluding shot, swords are stuck in
the tombs of dead samurai as chopsticks are placed in a
rice bowl to be offered to the dead.

"That kind of sword represents traditionalism," Kato
said pointedly, "the traditional feelings of the Japanese
people toward the dead. So Kuronuma was seeking a return to tradition. His subsequent films do not interest me
at all."

It struck Judith that only she was aware of the *non
sequitur*. No one seemed to expect logic or a rational argument. Kato concluded by asserting that other Japanese
directors, left nameless, challenged traditional Japanese
ways of life and by so doing depicted the mentality of the
Japanese people much more clearly than Kuronuma ever
had. "They are our true artists," he finished, sitting down
looking highly pleased with himself.

Koshima was next, having not-so-subtly been introduced by Kato as one of those "true artists." His personal elegance immediately placed him in another realm
from that of his fellow Japanese panelists. Judith now felt
as if she had been desensitized, as if all the nerve endings
of feeling from her face to her feet had been deadened.

"I was at first very perplexed to be asked to be one of
the panelists here," said Koshima. "In her conclusion Miss
Frank said that Japanese filmmakers are immersed in the
history and social structure of Japan. It seems she has a
very simplistic understanding of the matter, and from
beginning to end this is her persistent error."

It would have been foolish not to have expected Koshima to retaliate. Judith braced herself, although her posture could not have been more rigid. She would not react to Koshima's assault.

"She is only interested in directors who illustrate the class structure of Japan," Koshima continued, tired, exasperated with the pointlessness of entering into such conversations with foreigners. She tried to remember what in her remarks Koshima was referring to. She had said that the social and cultural institutions of postwar Japanese society continue to perpetuate feudal ideas. Could she have expressed herself simplistically? Had Koshima deliberately oversimplified what she said?

"It has come to the point," Koshima went on, "that when one tries to understand a foreigner, one is always ensnared in a fundamental error."

She heard the word "foreigner" ring through the hall echoing back silent approbation, a reaction from the audience at last. She saw Paul Meredith place another cigarette in his lapis holder, as if he could not possibly be included in this term of abuse. She tried to regain her composure by remembering the Kuronuma films she had always loved, those about people with the will to violate those traditions which repressed their spirits, people refusing to conform to the status quo.

"If you ask people here," insisted Koshima, "Kuronuma is considered to be a most unlikely Japanese."

She smiled. She had heard it before. Kuronuma's great sin for many Japanese was that his films pleased the foreigners.

"I agree with Mr. Kato. The world Kuronuma returned to is actually one of tradition. I think this is why the popularity of Kuronuma's films increased."

Now he began to embellish. Kuronuma, he explained to his young audience, appealed only to the old, the stodgy, the conservative, to those entrenched in things as they were before the war.

Judith sighed. If given the chance, should she continue to argue that Kuronuma's films were about realizing oneself, even if it meant breaking with oppressive tradition? But Koshima had sat down, leaving the field to moderator Saito, whose five books had disappeared. One of them, she would learn much later, was a sycophantic study of Koshima himself.

Saito did not begin by agreeing with Koshima. This would be too obvious, too much a matter of gleeful consensus. Instead, he, too, chose to ally himself with Kato.

"Mr. Kato, I believe," said Saito, "pointed out most of the things I wanted to mention."

Saito then worked his way back to the point at which Kato and Koshima had met. "Kuronuma is, of course, essentially a traditionalist. After *My Life to Live* Kuronuma abandoned his aim of challenging Western culture with the spiritualism of the Japanese."

Judith was startled to hear Saito admitting that Kuronuma was at least *once* something of a rebel. But Saito, unaware that he had contradicted himself, recognized no point of agreement with the foreign intruder.

She felt like crying now. She saw herself assailed and isolated, most unfairly attacked. Could this, she thought, be what journalist Harada had in mind when he told the audience he hoped they would respond to the meeting with "depth of feeling"? The other panelists were indeed paddling in a sea of feeling. She alone was caught in an undertow. Obviously they wished she would drown, disappear, cease to disturb their placid world. Kuronuma had been only the nominal subject of the attack upon a foreign critic. Powerless to reverse the tide, she lost any capacity to withstand its currents. Beset by a cabal of sharklike male opponents, she foundered. Finally invited by Saito to respond to what had been said, for a moment she lost the thread of the argument entirely.

Then she rallied. "I am offended to be described as a foreigner because I disagree with Mr. Koshima," she said heatedly. "I admit, however, that I cannot know as much about Japanese culture, literature or society as he."

She struggled for the calm to return to the subject of Kuronuma. "It has been said that Kuronuma really celebrates tradition. I cannot find very much evidence of this. Let us examine the last scene of *The Samurai of the Camellias*, to be shown later this evening. Tradition is indeed restored. But Kuronuma is passionate in his evocation of how this confines and distorts the community. The chamberlain who is rescued by the samurai of the camellias is a political man, selfish in his power, jealous of the samurai whose open heart and skill make him the only leader worthy of the people. The tradition that is restored is inferior to the independent spirit of the Kuronuma hero."

She addressed herself to Saito. As moderator, wouldn't he at least, if only in the interest of objectivity, allow her to regain a vestige of credibility?

"I don't understand," she said, "what is meant by Kuronuma's 'spiritualism.' Perhaps I'm wrong, but it appears that Mr. Saito equates 'spiritualism' with a challenge to Western culture. Kuronuma does make this challenge, but why call his opposition to Westernization 'spiritual'?"

Even as she spoke she recognized that addressing herself to a semantic problem was a mistake. She began to talk so rapidly that her words rushed forth in a barely articulated flurry. How could the interpreters be coping with this? Then she would hesitate and to her own ear her sentences sounded disjointed. She began to use too many "maybes" and "perhapses," trying to placate her foes with tentative language. This attempt at appeasement made the others even angrier.

Barely able to contain himself, Saito retorted, "I, of course, used the word 'spiritualism.' I'm afraid the situation is the same with you, Miss Frank. You may feel that many of the words we use are ambiguous. But we feel the same way about you. When I used the word 'spiritualism,' I took it for granted that everybody understood its meaning. If you ask me what I really mean by this word, I find it very difficult to explain it explicitly."

Once again the Japanese panelists had demonstrated that national differences made communication impossible.

His turn having rolled around again, Kato sententiously picked up where Saito left off. "There is a misunderstanding about concepts between us. But even if we find some consensus in this room, it would not mean much. It may be helpful in this type of session if we accept disagreement, even some misunderstanding."

The implication, she saw, was that if there was bad feeling, it was she alone who had occasioned it. The audience was being encouraged to embrace misunderstanding as the only possible outcome of such an event.

"The Nippon Company where Kuronuma began," Koshima was now saying in the monotone he hoped would conceal his irritation, "represented large capital and tried to initiate nonfeudal filmmaking. Kuronuma became Western and unlike the Japanese. So he seems to take up concepts of 'good' and 'love' in a Western manner. He believes it is possible for Japanese to be 'good' and to 'love' in the Western sense."

Judith realized she had stopped listening when she

heard Koshima mention "love." She wondered what it meant to love in the Western sense. Did it mean commitment to a woman as an individual? Was there a Western style of lovemaking that was alien to the Japanese? She allowed her mind to wander, having been deserted by her will. The voices droned on.

The program concluded with Saito requesting a closing comment from each of the panelists.

"I have felt frustrated," Judith found herself saying. "We've spent a long time together, but I don't think we've understood each other at all."

Even while she was speaking she knew this was the worst possible note on which to end. The moment had come to resolve differences, to expand upon how enlightening the meeting had been, to be grateful for how much insight she had gained into the film world of Japan, despite or even because of their differing points of view.

But she was paralyzed by the subtle cohesion by which the others had joined hands. The more they invoked sincerity, twisting and turning all the while to continue the attack on Kuronuma, if for no better reason than that she had praised him, the less able she was to do anything except back away from their coldness.

His final opportunity for comment at hand, Koshima could barely contain himself.

"I wonder whether there was any point at all to this panel discussion," he said. "I'm sorry to have used the word *foreigner* and sorry that she is mad at me. But when we speak about Japan and the Japanese, I would like to know what internal motive Miss Frank has. I can hardly understand with what motivation she speaks of Japan and the Japanese. If possible I would like Miss Frank to explain this. On what basis are you interested in the Japanese or in Japan?" he repeated, still without glancing in her direction. "I cannot imagine this from what you have said here."

She suddenly felt so cold, so numb that she thought she had been buried in ice. Did she need a motive to be studying either Japanese film or the films of Kuronuma, or, for that matter, the films of Koshima himself? He had used the term *internal motive*. Was the redundancy for emphasis or to underline his indignation? Was his inspiration paranoid, suggesting that her motive had been to attack *him* and in this manner rehabilitate the tired reputation of Kuronuma, now so clearly out of favor with Japanese film critics? Would he have challenged the motives of anyone who did not come to praise him?

By raising the issue of "internal motives," Koshima was suggesting that she had been flaunting Western superiority. Westerners praised Kuronuma because he was an Uncle Tom rejecting his own venerable traditions in favor of the spurious individualism of which the West was so self-righteously proud. No matter that Koshima had himself rejected those same traditions as stultifying and preventing a postwar revitalization of Japanese culture. The foreigner had not properly paid obeisance *to him*. Disingenuously he must accuse her of racism, of studying the Japanese as if they were some primitive tribe whose traditions were in need of cataloguing. By "internal motive" he might even have been implying that she had been sponsored by the American State Department, by the CIA itself, to spy on *him*.

Gasping as the last vestige of cordiality disappeared, she could respond only lamely. "I'm not one of those people who come to Japan in search of the exotic. I don't understand why Mr. Koshima should question the motives of a foreigner coming to Japan to study."

Then, she added, "Perhaps it is he who is insecure."

This last turned out to be the red flag flagrantly waved at a bull temporarily at bay. Koshima rose out of turn to renew his attack. "I'm not insecure," he all but shouted, "but I'm very interested in knowing what internal motive you have toward Japan and the Japanese."

He mentioned a book about Japan written in the twenties by a Chinese whose motive in analyzing the Japanese was his fear that China was about to be invaded by Japan.

"Of course, I do not expect such a contribution from you, Miss Frank." He leered. "But we are very interested in why you have been studying Japan."

Kato's summation was succinct. "I am in entire agreement with Mr. Koshima."

Saito soon brought the meeting to its merciful close. But first he added a reference to Kuronuma's suicide attempt, a delicate subject which she had not expected to be mentioned at all. But Saito had a motive of his own. "We Japanese panelists," he declared, "would like to say at this time that we feel sorry for what has happened to Mr. Kuronuma and that we share his sorrow."

The foreigner was excluded from the circle of good feeling, as if she were scarcely human at all. No matter that it was she who had spent the afternoon praising the great films of Kuronuma, and they who had belittled them.

She looked quickly at the spot where Paul Meredith had been standing. But her isolation, her loneliness were complete; he had vanished. As the afternoon had worn on, she had hoped that however awkward their previous meetings, he, the only other foreigner here, would have sympathized with her. Living in Japan so many years he must often himself have been excluded by the Japanese without explanation as they closed ranks against the alien presence in their midst. She had been able to hold on, she realized, only because he would be there when it was all over.

She had counted on the comfort of their knowing each other, of their both being outsiders here, even of their speaking the same language. She had needed him, and he had fled into the night. Maybe he felt her raw, newly arrived foreignness might condemn him in the eyes of the others. But after this ordeal, how she needed a friend! Well, he wasn't to be the one. She wondered if she would ever see him again. Japan, a little island, was packed with human beings. It was doubtful that they would meet.

The final words had been spoken. The panelists stood and faced the audience. The Japanese panelists bowed. She inclined her head to make the gesture, refraining from actually bowing so as not to appear to be conceding to the propriety of their personal attacks on her. No matter. The audience had been granted no opportunity to ask questions or to express opinions. No one seemed aware that this in itself was another indication that Kuronuma in his respect for individual judgment remained far ahead of his time. And no doubt these young people, schooled in obeisance to authority, would have been too shy to stand up and ask questions, let alone express disagreement with what such important figures as Koshima, Kato, and Saito had to say.

The sea of faces which had looked up at her for three hours remained expressionless. The panelists now drifted off the stage, the Japanese ahead, engaged in animated conversation, she alone, trailing behind. The *Nichinichi*, milking every drop of advantage from the occasion, had arranged for her to be interviewed by one of the radio stations they owned. When she was alone again, the hallways were completely deserted. Saito had long since departed, the books he had offered to her tucked under his arm. No one had uttered a word of farewell.

Part Two

Chapter One

She fled Kyoto the next morning. A sour aftertaste
poisoned every moment. She couldn't wait to
leave Japan. She would never come back. She hoped she
would never see any of those people again. But there was
not much danger of that. Their victory was complete.

Bitter and alone back in Tokyo, she dragged herself
to obligatory tourist attractions: Ueno Park, the Meiji
Shrine, the Kabuki Theater. In Asakusa she was molested
from behind by a man with wispy gray hair, a khaki work-
shirt, and high rubber boots. The man persistently
hovered in her trail, as if once was not enough. When she
complained to her guide, the woman, bored, put upon,
pretended not to understand her. She let the matter drop,
but watched warily from the corner of her eye as the man
monitored her movements, concealing himself behind little
booths selling cheap trinkets and greasy fried food.

Then, with only a few days of her stay left, she
received a call from a man identifying himself as Kuronuma's representative. Would she like the opportunity to
interview the great director? They were sorry they had
not contacted her before, but Kuronuma had been ill.

She was elated; this she hadn't expected, a chance to
meet Kuronuma himself! She spent a sleepless night, too

excited even to fantasize. The meeting was to take place in the lobby of the Imperial Hotel, impersonal and yet intimate, with its little nooks and alcoves where throughout each day businessmen sat, gin and tonic in hand, and where Arab sheiks were greeted with deep bows by Japanese executives.

In the morning a secretary phoned to say that Kuronuma would not come alone. With him would be a woman who was his close friend; obviously she alone was trusted to interpret. Also included in the group would be Paul Meredith, whose presence no doubt reflected mandatory protocol because he had written the only book about Kuronuma in English.

Her heart sank when she heard that Paul Meredith would be at her interview with Kuronuma. He despised her. He probably would revel in the fact that his presence alone—without his having to utter a word—would so throw her off balance that any frank communication, any touching of the soul of Kuronuma, any chance she had of letting him know how deeply she appreciated his work, would be utterly lost to her. It was ruined before it began. The very sound of Paul Meredith's name dampened her spirits.

She went down to the lobby much too early. Kuronuma's friend was the first to appear. The woman seemed to be making sure to be there before Kuronuma to spare him the unpleasant trial of meeting a foreign critic without a buffer. Paul Meredith arrived next, only half-attempting to conceal his ironic smile with a show of cordiality. He sat down next to Judith on the leather banquette, a young-old man come to cast a pall over the morning, one of those ghosts of indeterminate age and sex out of the Kabuki come to take the living to task for transgressions they had long since forgotten.

Before Kuronuma arrived, another man appeared, tall for a Japanese, displaying broad white teeth in a smile that seemed to fill his entire face. He was the producer of Kuronuma's new film, and his name was Mr. Matsushita. As he handed Judith his card, he declared, quickly yet formally, that if he could be of any service to her, she was certainly to call him. Mr. Matsushita projected a sense of friendly accessibility, a directness. He seemed incapable of the dance of evasion perfected by most of the people she had met in Japan. She wondered vaguely what help he could possibly be, since she was interested in speaking only with Kuronuma himself.

The woman now expressed her fear that Kuronuma might not spot them. Yet she did not want to have him paged. He would hate being recognized by nosy onlookers. And then Kuronuma walked into the lobby, greeting first the woman who was his friend, then Paul Meredith, toward whom he displayed the same ironic coolness Paul had shown Judith. Mr. Matsushita he seemed not to notice at all.

The interview was brief. Kuronuma said he was perplexed by the panel discussion, an excerpted version of which he had read in the *Nichinichi*. He didn't say why. He was pleasant and friendly enough as he responded to Judith's questions, but he repeated almost verbatim remarks quoted in Paul Meredith's book published eight years before. Paul and Mr. Matsushita sat on an adjoining banquette deeply engaged in conversation. They appeared not to be listening to the dialogue between Judith and Kuronuma. The single new piece of information Judith managed to extract, hardly startling or conclusive, was that Kuronuma planned to make a film about pollution.

She found herself staring at the diagonal white scars around Kuronuma's throat, the result of the suicide at-

tempt Mr. Saito had invoked at the close of the panel discussion in Kyoto and that Paul Meredith had recounted so
lasciviously in New York. And before she could devise a
way of outwitting Kuronuma's methodical repetition of
comments he had made to critics through the years, the
woman announced, "Mr. Kuronuma must be getting
tired." The interview was over.

Then something altogether unexpected happened.
The three Japanese departed together after farewells that
seemed warm with relief that the ordeal with the foreigner
was over. She was left alone with Paul.

"Shall we have lunch?"

She was amazed. Didn't he despise her, hadn't he
mocked her unprepared, uninformed, precipitous rush
into battle with Japanese culture? Didn't he find her unseemly? Why was he lingering now?

He took her arm as they made their way out onto the
Ginza through this, the New Wing of the Imperial Hotel
which she now knew was the main lobby, well-known as a
gathering place for meetings. Perhaps he had legitimately
expected her to be aware of this the last time they had
met. She felt now that at last he had become the same man
whose lyrical voice had described the wonders of Kuronuma's art in the book which she and many others had
believed the best study of a film director ever written.

"I love your book about Kuronuma," she told him.
"I've read it over so many times I almost know it by
heart."

He allowed her to praise him without interjecting a
disingenuous cutting remark that would accuse her of flattery, or of wanting something for herself. She felt that this
time he was taking the trouble to see her as she was, as the
moment captured her. She could relax and be herself.

"He didn't tell you very much today," Paul said sympathetically. "But compared to the way he treats *Japanese* critics, he was extremely friendly. You did very well. He never was much good at articulating what he 'meant to say' in his films. I'm not sure he ever meant to say very much."

She felt he was trying to buoy her spirits, place the occasion in its context. She had not done badly. It was a victory that Kuronuma had seen her at all.

"I wanted to ask him about the transitional moments in his films, the end of one era and the beginning of another, when human beings find themselves caught up in history. . . ." Her voice trailed off. Would he think her pretentious?

"He wasn't about to let you get into that!"

She told him her feelings about the panel discussion. He focused his anger at Koshima.

"Now *he* has ideas," said Paul. "But he doesn't know much about filmmaking."

Warmed by his accessibility, she let herself experience what had happened to her here. "I think I hate Japan," she confessed. "How do you manage to survive here?"

How did he? Now he was no longer the manipulative Paul Meredith against whom she had been warned, but the only person who could understand the pain she felt Japan had inflicted upon her.

"The Japanese are fanatics," said Paul. "They tolerate me out of a sense of superiority. I seem to believe myself rational, so I clearly must be less civilized. For acquiescing in this fantasy I'm rewarded, invited to the best parties."

With his sophistication and breeding, Paul could pull

this off; she couldn't. Today he was so open about himself that she couldn't imagine why she had ever been in awe of him. Here they were in a nondescript cafe, with no name on the door, no identity, eating enormous juicy hamburgers splashed liberally with Heinz ketchup. They were the best hamburgers in Tokyo, he told her.

He would be a guide to the best of everything.

"I'll never come back," she said fiercely.

He had smiled, his eyes dancing, benignly reassuring. She felt he thought she was right. And hadn't he closed one of his books with just that line, "I don't care if I never go back"? He had understood her.

Of the people present at the interview with Kuronuma, she had barely noticed Mr. Matsushita at all. Yet, alone in her room the following morning, she felt as if she had seen him somewhere before, his face looked so familiar. Then she remembered. Preparing for this trip, she had read a book about Japanese art. There in a late sixteenth-century painting of a feudal *daimyo* she had seen what could have been an exact likeness of Mr. Matsushita.

The portrait was that of a warrior holding a fan, a sword by his side. His face was heavily lined, his eyebrows slightly raised. He seemed a man who had witnessed—or executed—every human travail. Competent, self-satisfied, a man who had made his will felt. There was also a sensitivity about him, as if he were secreting a private softer self capable of the finest discriminations.

She felt she wanted to see Mr. Matsushita again, half-consciously believing that here lay her last chance for closeness with a Japanese. Through Mr. Matsushita, so uncannily resembling that sixteenth-century warrior lord, she could reach the true Japan.

She found the white card he had presented to her so formally. Not a business card at all, it turned out to contain only his name and personal number. Feeling reckless, she dialed it. A sleepy, muffled voice replied, then at once became more alert. Mr. Matsushita invited her to dinner the following night, the day before she was to leave Japan.

Dressed casually in a white long-sleeved shirt and dark trousers, Matsushita arrived exactly on time. He seemed smaller than he had during the interview with Kuronuma, less self-confident, unsure of where to go, what to do. His demeanor suggested a man in need of protection, of comfort, although he seemed one who would never openly request solace. Every inch of his being begged that he be understood, treated softly, kindly. Judith felt at ease. He was so clearly trying to please her.

After they had sat in the hotel lobby for half an hour, Matsushita proposed that they visit the Chinese quarter of Yokohama. They would have dinner at the very restaurant frequented by Kuronuma when he had shot a film in that city. Sitting by his side as he drove swiftly through the tunnel linking Tokyo with Yokohama, Judith was conscious of his attractiveness.

He parked his car in an expensive lot. Carefully he paid the fee and deposited the ticket in his pocket. Then he led her down the narrow alley of restaurants. She felt safe with him.

At first they talked about Kuronuma, the one subject they knew they had in common. Matsushita understood English very well, but found speaking so tiring that he confined himself to the obvious, allowing sharp, perceptive glances at the right moment to convey all he knew and felt.

"Which of Kuronuma's films are your favorites?"

She named the one about the peasants and the samurai, which was attacked with such fervor by Kato, and another about a civil servant who learns he has stomach cancer and seeks to make his wasted life count in the months remaining to him.

Matsushita nodded approvingly, indicating that their taste was the same. She relaxed. Good feeling seemed to billow out, enveloping them in a cloud of understanding. He trusted her. He didn't believe what Saito, Kato, and Koshima implied, that she had come to Japan with hostile ulterior motives. He was Japanese and she was a foreigner, but they were one in how they assessed the vanities of this world. She felt he appreciated the purity of her soul, her innocence, that he saw her value. He put his arm around her shoulders as they walked. It was enough. For a moment it even seemed as if they had already made love and this was the morning after. Sexual tension rose and fell, flared up from within her and then receded. She hadn't been with a man for so long that she wasn't sure if the strong physical sensations she was experiencing were sufficient for her to let him know that she wanted him. Suppose she were wrong and he was simply being polite to a foreigner who had admired Kuronuma only to be met with disdain by Japanese film critics. How was she to know if he felt desire for her? His smile itself seemed to penetrate her, but was he only being flirtatious? Did he intend that they should actually touch each other? She who had lost the sense of her own body could not figure out whether he would wish to make love to her. And so she failed in her effort to conjure up the image of their being naked together. Lacking the image, she lost the reality. He seemed open and close and yet distant, other, Japanese. It had been too long. Now her only hope was in him. Perhaps he would make the decision, place his hands upon her more firmly, sweep her into the certainty that he could love her as she was.

They entered Yokohama's Chinatown. She had no interest whatever in where Kuronuma ate his lunch when he was filming here eight years ago, but they had to have a destination. This was as good as any. Kuronuma had brought them together, and so it was fitting that in homage they should retrace the artist's steps. Did Matsushita know that she called only because she wanted to be with him and not because she was accumulating otherwise inaccessible data about Kuronuma's habits of work? But until she was sitting beside Matsushita in his car speeding away from Tokyo, she hadn't even allowed herself to feel how attracted she was to him.

They arrived too late. In the very narrow room that was Kuronuma's favorite restaurant a heavy woman sitting at a table gestured angrily toward the door. The place was closed. Matsushita shrugged in disappointment and led Judith across the street to an enormous, Hong Kong-like palace festooned with red paper lanterns. The walls were fake red enamel gilded with gold paint. *This place* would be open all night. Although there was an English-language version of the menu, Matsushita did all the ordering, rapidly indicating a dish from virtually every page—pork, shrimp, duck in plum sauce, thick shark's fin soup.

She self-consciously ate and ate. Matsushita, whose body seemed all vein and sinew, wiry muscle and distended nerves, sat watching her. It seemed he had had his dinner at some earlier hour. But it was not his nature to make so rude or gratuitous an admission. He looked into her eyes while she coped clumsily with slippery ivory chopsticks dyed red.

Then in a low mournful voice, barely a whisper, Matsushita began to reveal details of his personal life. She was startled. No Japanese had spoken to her so intimately. Was it his insufficient command of spoken English or the extraordinary nature of the moment that led Matsushita in rapid, disjointed sentences to tell her the history of his affections?

"I'm divorced," he confided.

"Isn't that unusual for someone of your generation?" She knew that it was. Japanese men invariably had mistresses but rarely absented themselves legally, inextricably, from the continuities of home and hearth. Yet she was elated by this turn in the conversation. The more Matsushita deviated from traditional Japanese ways, the more likely he was to reach out to a foreigner. And what an unlikely Japanese he was, to feel that only a foreigner could truly understand him.

"I have a son, but I haven't seen him for years. He's eleven now. My wife is the intermediary. She lets him know how I feel. I didn't want to confuse him," Matsushita said, smiling helplessly.

Her eyes filled with tears. She felt an overpowering yearning, as if she wanted to take him in her arms and comfort him. It was he who had suffered most for having relinquished the right to know his son.

"You must see him, he needs you," she insisted. It became important to her that Matsushita open his arms to his lonely son, bereft of a father who loved him but who had chosen to punish himself by withholding that love.

"I keep in close touch," Matsushita added quickly. "I had lunch with my wife only today." He blushed at the slip. "I mean, my ex-wife."

Was it his English which had betrayed him or his

feelings? At once she saw his wife as a firmly entrenched rival. Was he intentionally, ironically, drawing boundaries for her?

They drove to a hilltop overlooking the bright lights of teeming, hysterical Yokohama, where music blared through the night and life was more frantic and urgent than elsewhere in Japan, as if the presence of the port, access to the outside, threw the Japanese into a frenzy. At a large white house, once the location of a Kuronuma set, Matsushita leaped over the fence and stood looking down at the life below. She lagged behind. Had he meant for her to join him in the dark? She didn't approach, longing now for a connection with Matsushita unrelated to Kuronuma.

In the car as they drove back to Tokyo he invited her to lunch the next day, her last. She sat close to him, feeling again that surging sexual desire. But she told herself, not now, there would be another time, she would make it happen. They hadn't built enough between them to accommodate this sexual desire, which surprised her since she had experienced no physical urge for Matsushita, surely, when she met him at the Imperial Hotel during the interview with Kuronuma. But he would be here for her later, this vibrant, alert man who seemed to be bearing the weight of the world on his narrow shoulders. He would remain available, he would not marry anyone. She knew she wanted him, but didn't know what to do, how to break down this last distance.

He walked her to her room, his arm around her shoulders. Neither said a word. It didn't occur to her that he might mistake her silence for alienation. She opened the door and when she turned to look down the long corridor after him, he had vanished. As soon as she was inside, she knew she had made a mistake. She had been a coward, too timid to risk breaking through their awkwardness. She had felt sweaty, unattractive. Why had she let him go? It was now discomforting to be compelled to embrace the emptiness with which she had so long fortified herself against the world.

And suddenly it was bitter that she had to leave inhospitable Japan the very next afternoon.

Their lunch was anticlimatic. Matsushita arrived half an hour late, profusely apologetic. Still without the courage to examine her feelings, she felt euphoric. Yet why was she leaving now that she had found so sympathetic a spirit? Had she become blindly obedient to the inevitable? At lunch they talked of Kuronuma. This was most comfortable, for of what else could they speak amid the publicity of the coffee shop of the Imperial Hotel?

Matsushita assumed he would be driving her to the airport. Sitting beside him again she felt as if she had known him forever. Now she was warm, relaxed, tender. She felt the happiness of being in his presence, holding back the pain of having to leave him for later. The distance to Haneda Airport seemed but the duration of a single striking of the clock. The more she tried to hold on to the time, the more it eluded her.

Matsushita said: "In a few days we will all be going to Kuronuma-san's villa for a summer holiday. It's a pity you have to leave."

But he never said "stay" and she was afraid to be so bold as to offer to change her plans, turn around, and come back. She had given up her hotel room. Where would she stay?

Matsushita murmured, "Judith, Judith." She looked at him expectantly, waiting for him to take responsibility, to invite her. She imagined Kuronuma's villa, she and Matsushita special guests there in a room of their own, at home and at one with the great artist, at the center of everything in this world that mattered.

Matsushita had fallen silent. Words were an impossible means of communication for them. Lost without her accustomed directness, she could only wait for a sign from him. But Matsushita would go no further and she had no alternative but to go home.

And alone in the Japan Airlines terminal she reminded herself of the work waiting, the book she wanted to write about her experiences in Japan.

Matsushita would wait while she made herself a stronger, more self-sufficient person, a woman who didn't throw her work to the winds out of longing for a man. When she was ready Matsushita would be there for her. She would come back.

Chapter Two

She fell into despondency in New York. Why had she deprived herself of affection? She hadn't counted on his staying in her mind, on the pain of having left their connection unfinished. But precisely because they hadn't quite touched, Matsushita became so real to her that there wasn't a day when she didn't think of him, relive their brief meetings, catalogue his every word, gesture, expression. Filled with longing, she saw that the book could have waited, it would have taken care of itself. Matsushita was the life she had caught a glimpse of in her ceaseless devotion to not living. He embodied her need long suppressed to return to a normal human existence. Twice she dreamed she was still on the plane. It had not yet cleared Tokyo Bay. She could still change her mind, return, and offer herself to him. It was bitter that she hadn't. And once she dreamed that Matsushita was on the airplane with her.

Before long she busied herself in work again, writing articles about Japan. She signed a contract to write a book about Japanese cinema. Matsushita was always in her thoughts, but she never questioned whether her decision to take on this ambitious project was connected with her yearning for him. Secretly, subconsciously, she saw the book as a love letter. In reading how she saw his world, he would understand, he would love her. By her perceptions of Japan, she would win his approval. It was like being six years old and feeling she could become valuable only if she were smart in school. Patterns persist. She lacked the physical grace which belonged to Matsushita in such abundance; she could never offer him so splendid a physical presence as he provided her. But their sensibilities would touch. And even if it took two years before she could return to him, she was certain he would still be free. He seemed in need of the consolation that only an outsider could provide, someone to whom he could unburden himself without the consequences of local exposure. He might even prefer a foreigner who could not herself put into the Japanese language the doubts he seemed in need of confessing.

Meanwhile she devoted herself to work, which included studying elementary Japanese. She emerged from the library with tome upon tome of Japanese history, art, and philosophy. Reading, note-taking, accumulating insights in spiral notebooks, she calmed down. Work again gave her safety, perspective. Thinking back on her time in Japan, she regretted that she hadn't been able to set a tone of equanimity at that panel discussion. It must have been her own fault that she had blundered into being cast in the role of enemy by people like Koshima with whom she might really have had much to share. But most of all she regretted that she hadn't said to Matsushita, the only man for whom she had felt sexual desire in years, "Are you asking me to stay?"

Other men did not interest her. The desire awakened by Matsushita was reserved only for him. Having withheld herself from physical connection, the sexual act had become sacred, a ritual of deliverance. She could now be open only to this man, the one she had freely chosen, who would be able to offer the ecstasy for which it would have been profoundly worth waiting.

Meanwhile she kept track of his whereabouts. Friends visiting Japan reported that he and Kuronuma were making a film in Siberia. Finally, two years after she left Japan, having gained Matsushita's address from a mutual friend passing through New York, she wrote him that she would be returning to do research on a book. She would very much like to see him. She never doubted that even if Matsushita were in Siberia, something would bring him back to Japan during her stay, which was to last for several months.

From Siberia, Matsushita promptly replied. His letter was brief, but warm and cordial. It announced that he would be home two weeks after Judith's arrival.

Elated, she whisked herself off to Japan. There those first two weeks she immersed herself in work, surrounded by so lovely an aura of expectancy that she was unusually calm. The inevitable misunderstandings, the result of failures of communication about the times of screenings, the unavailability of crucial prints, failed to rattle her as they undoubtedly would have if she had not been safe and secure in her cocoon of anticipation.

One morning at six, the victim of expectation more than jet lag, she dialed Matsushita's number, although it was still a week before he was scheduled to return to Tokyo. Why she did it, or what she sought, she couldn't say. But after four rings and just as she was about to replace the receiver, a woman sleepily replied.

Dismayed and yet aware that she really knew very little about Matsushita's personal life, she hung up. Was seeing him then a hopeless folly, her little nurtured fantasy? Yet he might have allowed someone not particularly close to him to stay in his apartment in his absence. An empty apartment didn't make sense in crowded Tokyo. But perhaps Matsushita was inaccessible, committed to other relations that left no room for her and about which she knew nothing.

Her expectations loosened. Now she wondered whether he would even call her upon his arrival.

Matsushita was to return to Tokyo on a Friday. He didn't call. On Saturday she deliberately scheduled a busy day: a double feature in the tiny art theater in Shinjuku which usually played Koshima's films, a visit to an art gallery, drinks in her room with a professor friend at six. The telephone rang at seven. One side of her had known that whether or not a woman was living in Matsushita's apartment with him, he would call. Yet she was shocked when she heard his voice. Had he tried earlier and found her absent? There had been no message. But Matsushita would simply have hung up and called again. To leave one's name bespoke vulnerability.

She asked him how he was.

"Very well. And you?"

"I'm fine," she all but shouted, intoxicated with gaiety.

"I'm very glad you've come back," he said warmly.

And then she became effusive, bubbling over with the excitement of talking to him at last. But after two years how could she admit why she was so happy? How could she tell him that she had loved and waited for him all this time? So she attributed her euphoria to her work. She was ecstatic at seeing four Japanese films a day, lining up interviews, collecting rare stills. She was immersed in her new book. She rattled on and on, demonstrating her self-sufficiency, taking pride in showing that she wanted but did not need him.

Matsushita was quiet. When he spoke again his tone had changed. He had become cold, pragmatic.

"Are you busy tomorrow?" he interrupted.

But she was. She had agreed to meet a documentary filmmaker named Ogawa to view his new film. The screening had been set up a week before; to cancel was unthinkable. The barbarity of such behavior would slide like mercury through the tightly knit film world. Koshima would hear about it and gloat, and she might find it difficult to meet other directors. Besides, now that Matsushita had called it wouldn't matter if they postponed meeting for a few more hours.

The expectation of seeing him remained delicious. Extending it by a few hours would make it more so. But suddenly she wondered if he believed her. She registered that his tone had changed. Rapidly, impersonally, he said, "I'll call you tomorrow at eleven." And he rang off.

Still, she settled into a peace, relieved to yield to Matsushita's taking control. From eleven to noon the next day she remained in her room, mildly disquieted by his failure to call. Perhaps she had misunderstood him, perhaps he had misunderstood her.

At noon she had to go on to her appointment.

The documentary filmmaker Ogawa kept offices in Shinjuku, far across town from the Ginza, remote from the world of Matsushita who worked in staid, commercial Akasaka.

A friendly young assistant opened the door. Mr. Ogawa hadn't arrived, but they could begin the film. It was a sympathetic examination of the dockworkers of Yo-kohama, nonunionized, abandoned people living on the periphery of Japan's prosperity. After a few minutes Ogawa, a pleasant-looking man with a sweet smile and warm, kind eyes, entered the tiny room and sat down, making enthusiastic comments as if he were enjoying the experience of filming anew.

Judith struggled to concentrate on the film and not to dwell on the image of Matsushita somewhere in the labyrinths of Tokyo. Could he already be lost to her?

Suddenly she became caught up in what Ogawa was saying. He was talking about his experience of actually living with the dockworkers, how finally it had become impossible for him and his crew not to intervene in their lives directly, encouraging them to abandon their passivity, not to accept life conditions which made them less than human.

He was virtually un-Japanese in the openness with which he expressed affection for the dockworkers, men without social identities. Some had no given names, only surnames. One had taken the name George, in homage to the black American G.I. who took care of him when he was orphaned and alone during the Occupation. Before that he had lived on garbage in Ueno Park. Ogawa valued them all for themselves, appearing in the film now and then as a sympathetic friend.

Since there was no money for coffins, the dead were wrapped in blankets. The community was so poor that they had only one funeral a year, mourning all those who had died during the past twelve months. The largest cause of death was accident on the job; the second, alcoholism. The life expectancy of these men was forty.

"When I shot the funeral scene," Ogawa confided,

"many people came up to me and said, 'I may die any day. Please take my picture so that there may be a picture of me at my funeral.'" For the moment allowing herself to forget the absent Matsushita, she felt the sadness of Ogawa's victimized people. Images of traditional Japanese funerals, during which well-fed mourners sat beneath a photograph of the deceased, flashed before her eyes.

Ogawa whispered, "That legless man asked me not to shoot his whole body." Ogawa said he had disobeyed. He explained that the handicapped were shunned in Japan, deformed people ostracized as if their very presence would undermine the prevailing order. Everything was dependent upon conformity, he said, consistency—the fulfilling of one's appointed role.

A man was asked how he had ended up in this district. "Because I wanted to have brothers." A moment later, on camera, he collapsed, unable to breathe. The crew continued to film as Ogawa called an ambulance and then rode along with him to the hospital. A shot later Ogawa and the man were chatting, the patient obviously feeling better. "This country is already changing," he said. "One day I hope it will change totally. What is needed is a revolution. Perhaps I will die before it happens."

In another scene the dockworkers learned that the mayor of Yokohama had received a New Year's bonus of five hundred thousand yen. "Why doesn't he come and serve us a cup of tea or something?" asked the sick man. "He should give us a part of his bonus and treat us to a bowl of noodles!"

"A union was finally formed," said Ogawa when the lights were turned on. "We had something to do with it. It hasn't much power; yet one sick man had previously been refused admission to the local hospital, but when a union member went with him, they had to back down."

Ogawa turned to Judith, his soft, pockmarked face full of patient good will. Shyly, without guile, he asked if she could stay to lunch. She was touched by his hospitality as they moved into an alcove just beyond the tiny screening room.

A table laden with a magnificent banquet seemed to have materialized out of nowhere. Hot and shimmering, cold and glistening, a multitude of dishes stood waiting, in hues ranging from pink, orange, iridescent green and gold and ivory to mauve and black. Fish, salads, pickles, sweets were delicately arranged in beautiful porcelain bowls. The sushi was elegantly modeled like finely composed sculpture. The entire banquet was a microcosm of the varieties of sensual experience. On this warm day there was chilled, shining bean curd prepared in the summer manner, kept cold in a container which possessed a compartment for ice in the summer heat and charcoal for winter. And there were tangy country dishes: duck stir-fried in fresh chrysanthemum leaves, long perfect slivers of red beef without a trace of fat, boiled rapidly in hot oil. The beauty of the food bespoke friendship and affection. Expressing life's bounty, it brought Judith and Ogawa close.

She was moved. A filmmaker like Ogawa was by studio standards, by Koshima's standards, obviously poor. But this feast was as elaborate as any she had been served in Japan.

Ogawa's staff members had meanwhile arrived, and everyone sat down to eat together. There was no sense of hierarchy, no awareness that Ogawa was more important than anyone else because he was "the director." If Judith felt uncomfortable at all, it was only when she observed that the women staff members who had cooked this lunch remained serving and working in the narrow galley kitchen. Relaxed, emboldened, she teased Ogawa: "Why aren't the women behind the cameras?" The men at the table laughed boisterously, but with a trace of nervousness. With a smile, Ogawa promised to explain later.

The afternoon wound down. Ogawa never spoke of the place of the women on his staff. Judith didn't reintroduce the question. It was obvious that Ogawa and his crew were not ready to accept Japanese women as equals to be trained in the technical side of filmmaking. But they had all treated Judith with respect, anxious to answer her questions and revealing no doubt that she would be able to convey their aims. They served her tea with cherry blossoms floating in it, a symbol of the good feeling of the day.

Ogawa walked her to the street and waited until a taxi arrived. Shyly she kissed him on the cheek and he smiled in surprise; his was a generation schooled in reticence.

The day had been suffused with purity. Leaving Ogawa to wait for Matsushita again, she wistfully said goodbye as well to her sane, true self.

Chapter Three

She returned to the hotel and rushed to the message desk. When she was told there were, in fact, no messages, she felt as if the bottom had dropped out of the world.

Unable to face her empty room, she had a drink with an American couple in the lobby. She feared the despair of not seeing Matsushita for whom she had waited all this time. Had she dreamed up his interest in her? Was it all a fantasy? She sat and allowed these strangers to cast her in the role of guide; she talked of food and where to buy the used kimonos Japanese brides would sell after they had been worn, gaudy red-and-white satin monstrosities decorated with gigantic hollyhocks with silver and gold thread stems. It was Sunday, and if Matsushita were not free today, who knew when he ever would be. Perhaps the woman who answered his telephone so sleepily was his ex-wife come home to her rightful place at last. Maybe she had never left the circle of Matsushita's responsibility and affection despite their divorce.

At seven the following evening, after she had spent the day at screenings, half-reconciled to missing him, Matsushita finally telephoned. His tone now was formal, the opposite of what it had been on Saturday. This time it was as if he were fulfilling an obligation and no more.

"My secretary arranged that I should see you on Tuesday," said Matsushita. "Is it possible to change it to Wednesday?"

Pained, despairing, trying desperately to be equally formal and determined to match him in unfriendliness, she replied coldly that she was free on Tuesday but had agreed to have dinner with someone else on Wednesday. Her eyes burned with unreleased tears.

Matsushita agreed to Tuesday, but sounded harried, as if he were being coerced. The conversation was as brief as it could be. If she had been free on Saturday would things have been different? It was impossible to say.

At six on Tuesday Matsushita called and said he would be a half-hour late. He would arrive at seven-thirty rather than seven. Numb now to his reluctance to see her, she waited in her room. At ten of eight she went down to the lobby and began compulsively to talk to a tall, suntanned man with a crew cut, handsome in the traditional sense, obviously a businessman lonely and eager to talk with an American woman. He contributed the requisite small talk, in which she acquiesced.

Buoyantly she kept up her part of the conversation, although the man was boring; he didn't interest her at all. But when Matsushita entered, she wanted him to see her with someone else, undaunted by his recalcitrance, independent, desirable to others. The American asked if he could call her; she said he could, having no intention of ever seeing him again.

Suddenly at a telephone she spotted a lean, sinewy man of indeterminate age wearing thick sunglasses. His hair was glossy and lush, brushed thickly back. He wore a maroon-and-gray tweed jacket over a black turtleneck sweater, as if he were an Italian gigolo out for a night on the town, not Japanese at all. Something about him suggested rapid movement, effectiveness, grace.

Was this Matsushita? Just by the manner in which he held the telephone this man seemed more assertive, at ease with life, less vulnerable than the one she had known. But it was Matsushita! Only like a chameleon he wore a new skin, smoother and even more sensuous than before. He also seemed more worldly, slightly dangerous.

These alterations paralyzed her so that she sat for a moment watching him call up to her room as if she were a spectator at a play. In that cathedral-sized lobby his beauty seemed so overwhelming that it was as if he had descended from a distant planet. She had to force herself to approach him.

Matsushita greeted her with that wide smile that unabandonedly exposed white teeth. She had purposely carried her briefcase, although it was hardly appropriate to a night out on the Ginza. She would use it as a shield, to protect herself so that it wouldn't be the woman Matsushita was encountering, but the writer. She would treat this as a businesss meeting, as if there were no feelings involved, as if she didn't want anything from him. She would show him articles about Kuronuma; she would ask his advice and so prove that she wasn't looking for a personal relationship.

She still had the hope that they might drive somewhere as they had on that first evening two years before; that the intimacy of the automobile would bring them together once again.

But Matsushita had this time parked his car in the hotel lot, determining that they walk to their destination.

This was to be a hostess bar on the Ginza frequented by movie people. She hadn't eaten dinner nor did he ask if she had.

They walked the short distance without speaking, wending their way down the thickly populated streets until they came to a nondescript building facing a dark alley. Matsushita opened the door and they climbed up a narrowly steep flight of stairs. The building bore neither name nor number on the door, admitting only favored patrons, particular acquaintances of the proprietress.

At the door the beaming Mama-san, a tall, beautiful woman in her late forties, greeted Matsushita with little shrieks of surprise and delight, half-teasing, half-seductive, as if he were a long-lost lover.

"Where have you been all this time?" she crooned. "I haven't seen you for ages."

Matsushita patiently described how he had been producing a film outside the country.

The woman seemed everything Judith could never hope to be—willowy, self-confident, elegant. The subdued lavender kimono she chose as befitting her years made her seem more rather than less vibrant. Her black hair, unflecked by gray, was pulled back in a chignon; her face was so heavily made up that her eyes seemed like two black marbles suspended in a creamy pink-and-white emulsion. Her presence was at the same time understated and commanding.

The Mama-san continued her symphony of greeting, half-reprimand, half-delight at the return of her naughty, wayward admirer who had foolishly been absent for so long from this sanctuary of the spirit. Matsushita smiled, coyly making his explanations. Judith retreated before the woman's radiance.

The entire bar was a room barely nine by twelve, but this Mama-san obviously cultivated her little garden with finesse and determination. Throughout the evening, without a shadow of irritation on her placid face, she divided her attentions among the groups of men seated at her little tables while younger surrogates assisted in the more menial tasks of serving.

It was obvious that Matsushita would have frequented this bar which she had noticed was only five minutes away from the Nippon Company. She also knew that Kuronuma had been Nippon's mainstay for many years until they decided he was no longer commercial and withdrew their support. Behind them four stocky, red-faced men were engaged in loud, animated conversation. Suddenly, just after they had been seated, Matsushita sprang from his seat and bounded over to their table like a gazelle. Judith turned around in time to catch him bowing to each of the men. In return he was awarded grunts of cordiality, bows, laughs of mutual recognition. No doubt they were inquiring after the well-being of Kuronuma, although they might be the very people who had made it so difficult for Kuronuma to continue making films in Japan. Equanimity at any cost. Not one looked her way, as if they didn't acknowledge that she, the only woman customer, was even in the room.

The Mama-san came over to ask if she would like to hang up her trench coat. But she kept it on. She felt large, awkward, although the red silk print dress embossed with tiny flowers was her favorite. The neckline seemed too low, too revealing, an inappropriate offering to an indifferent Matsushita. The color was again too loud; would she ever learn? She shrank before the beauty of the Mama-san who, ten years her senior, looked as a woman should.

While Matsushita talked to the film luminaries beyond, Judith remained alone, still holding on to the briefcase now on her lap, trying to settle herself in a seat that was clearly too narrow, behind an extremely slender table. And all the while the Mama-san exuded willed euphoria, like a fragrant liqueur that could be greedily imbibed by tired men in quest of a harmless, quick, and temporary relaxant.

Matsushita returned. He must have made a sign, because at once they were served many tiny dishes containing the delicacies that were the specialty of the house. The filet mignon was no doubt selected to please the foreigner vulgarly addicted to an excessive consumption of red flesh. There was also a stringy, semiliquid substance which Matsushita urged her to sample: "This one is made from potatoes." It seemed impossible to consume with chopsticks, but Matsushita delicately tasted it, as he did all the little plates. She couldn't touch any of the food.

The conversation moved slowly and awkwardly.

"How was the weather in Siberia?" she asked him.

Matsushita complained of how difficult it was to reach the shooting site from Japan. He'd had to take a plane, then a train, then drive for ten hours in the snow.

"Have you been working hard?" he asked her. She told him of the films she had seen, directors she had met.

"When will your book be finished?" His English seemed more taut and finely honed. He said nothing personal about himself. He didn't even inquire what she planned to say about Kuronuma's films in her book. Depths of silence stood like clouds between them.

Increasingly ill at ease, she opened her briefcase as if she were groping for her very self, buried in a compartment of papers. She drew forth notes garnered from Japanese sources about the film Matsushita was producing for Kuronuma. She had even had the script translated into English. She passed it to Matsushita as evidence of her serious intentions. Glancing quickly through the sheaf of papers, he made no comment.

"The reference in the script to evil Chinese is very odd," she said. "Did the Russians force Kuronuma to include this?"

Now Matsushita smiled, as if he had reached a high point of land, safety at last. She was speaking like any nosy journalist, domestic or foreign.

"Some student groups here made much of it, but the whole argument is senseless."

She wished she could tell him that she understood, that she sympathized. He, of course, was right. Politics was meaningless, transitory, the seeming capitulation of Kuronuma to the politics of his Soviet coproducers amounted to no more than a day's sound and fury, of no moment in the eternal order of things. And here was a weary Matsushita preoccupied with seeing that Kuronuma had all the necessary props and equipment, not to mention the required heavy undergarments for frigid Siberia where he was making his first film in five years.

She hesitated, then moved forward. After all, Matsushita's needs were one thing, the truth another. He obviously cared nothing for her. Why should she take into account the trials and tribulations of his self-inflicted role as Kuronuma's producer?

"But did the Russians actually change the script?" she pursued, anxious to salvage some unique detail from an otherwise perfunctory evening in which Matsushita was doing no more than fulfilling an obligation.

"No, those references were in the original story."

She didn't believe him. But to duplicate his neutrality, she chose a safer question.

"Is Kuronuma as skillful at his craft as he once was?"

To this Matsushita replied with a clipped affirmation. "Yes, he is!"

And so it went. Even as they made pretenses of conversation she couldn't free herself of the discomfort brought on by the very place as the Mama-san and her beautiful assistants, sylphlike beings in pale yellow kimonos, moved like shadows to and fro. Her coat slipped from her shoulders, but she held it around her. She must prove to Matsushita that she was no more involved in the evening than he. If she were violating the unspoken segregation of women from this refuge so clearly designed for the relaxation of men, it was for the sake of her work alone. The price of entering this male sanctuary was that she would not be considered a woman. Despite the red silk dress which had always made her feel sensual and alive, she felt without gender.

The silences lengthened. Finally, no longer able to be careful, she asked Matsushita why he didn't call back on Sunday morning as he had promised. "I was very angry with you," she half-teased.

There was nothing to lose, no reason not to attempt to penetrate the shell of Matsushita's cordial indifference. He smiled and affected the world-weariness which for him was as natural a defense as the spoken lie would be for someone who had faith in the verbal.

"I had so many things to do."

The topic died, as had all the others.

The Mama-san approached and whispered something to Matsushita which Judith could barely understand, something about what a bouncing, red-cheeked, pretty girl she was. They both laughed uninhibitedly. Judith tried to smile but succeeded only in shrinking back into her seat, feeling less and less herself. The Mama-san moved off to another table to join those guests in the pointedly subtle small talk at which she was so adept.

"Shall we go?" Matsushita inquired politely.

Gratefully, Judith rose.

They made their way back toward the Imperial Hotel, walking slightly apart from each other, retracing their steps down the same narrow Ginza streets. When a jaunty-looking, middle-aged man in gray suit and bow tie passed beside them, Matsushita quickly bowed very deeply from the waist, not once, but twice. The man seemed to be a high official of the Nippon Company. Certainly he must have been Matsushita's superior, for instead of bowing he inclined his head so slightly that the movement was almost imperceptible. Matsushita was his inferior; he could be vaguely pleasant but no more. By the time he had completed his bow, Matsushita seemed almost to have clicked his heels together. Then each of the men resumed his way along the gaudy Ginza street where, at ten o'clock, the lights were already beginning to go out.

They neared the hotel garage.

"Shall we go somewhere else?" Matsushita asked.

She was incredulous. He had not seemed to enjoy himself. He had confided nothing personal about himself, exuded none of that earlier air of vulnerability. They drove to the student quarter, Shinjuku, where bars catering to the young stayed open much later.

In the place to which Matsushita led her, the music was deafening. Full-lipped androgynous waiters in tight black pants with their hair gently shaped around their faces moved rapidly about. She asked if they were boys or girls. Matter-of-factly Matsushita replied that they were boys. At a tiny table in a nook above a curving iron staircase they sat and stared at each other and ate ginkgo nuts. "Have you ever tried these?" Matsushita inquired. The music was so loud they could not talk, and after a while they returned to the hotel.

Then, just as they were parting at the main entrance, and to her great surprise, Matsushita kissed her softly on the lips. He hesitated, staring into her eyes. He seemed to want to move toward her. Was he waiting for her to make some sign that she wanted him? He stood for an instant as if suspended in space. Then, quickly, he said that he would call her on Friday.

She walked inside. Suddenly she understood he had indeed been waiting for her to expose her desire to spend the night with him. But she would not allow herself to succumb to regret. If Matsushita were merely shy, she was only postponing their physical reunion. She could look forward to it, anticipate.

During the next few days, as she half-watched her films, involuntarily she relived Matsushita's kiss, remembering the softness of his touch, how much feeling could penetrate a fleeting moment. She thought of him constantly, never attempting to understand why he seemed so romantic, relinquishing in advance the possibility of analyzing why she was so drawn to him. It was enough for her to rejoice in the nobility of his beauty, the aristocracy of line which followed his high cheekbones, the capacity for sensuality hinted at by his full lips, the perceptions hidden behind his wide-set, enormous dark eyes.

Matsushita did not call on Friday as he had promised. She went on working, telling herself it was not over yet. But she did call Paul Meredith. Perhaps he would help her to understand what had happened. She could trust him to interpret the underside of the Japanese psyche which Matsushita now seemed bent on displaying.

They met in the coffee shop of the Imperial Hotel. Good friends by now, there was no room for coyness or subterfuge. "There's a man I'm interested in," she began, "a Japanese man."

"Who is it?" Paul demanded greedily. She noticed that, despite his adoption of so many other Japanese ways (he even seemed to speak English with a Japanese accent), he retained his direct American manner.

She spoke the name: Matsushita. What could she do? She had to give herself away even if it meant Paul's disapproval, even if this choice diminished her in his eyes.

"So it's *him*!"

He stopped. He would not judge.

"I've known him for years. He was always the odd boy at parties. He was so pretty. He always came late and he always came alone."

What could he mean by "the odd boy?" Was Paul implying that Matsushita was not heterosexual? Had Paul had his own encounters with him? But now Paul seemed barely able to contain his interest. That Matsushita was the man Judith craved drew her close to Paul in a new way.

Yet even the last time she had felt sympathetic vibrations between them. He had known when she had told him she would never come back that she would. That had begun their unspoken understanding. A strange intimacy seemed to be developing before her eyes. Paul was to be something for her. And she knew here in this coffee shop what it was. She was to be the prizefighter, encountering open combat in a manner he feared for himself. Her antagonist, his as well, was Japan; Paul would be her coach, instructing her in how the walls of this impenetrable culture might be undermined, in how a foreign woman might approach a Japanese man. She would stand in the front lines attacking indifference, xenophobia, insecurity; he would be right there behind her all the time, chief tactician in this war. "So it's *him*!" had been their starting bell, round one.

Warming to her first opportunity to discuss Matsushita with anyone, relieved that this was not to be her struggle alone, she told him everything. Paul listened.

"You must make the first move," he declared.

"Why must I?"

But she was only pretending. Effort could only heighten the connection with Matsushita when it finally happened.

"It can't be helped. The only way you can have him is by throwing him down on the bed."

The image fit. The robust Judith might easily push the wispy, lean Matsushita into submission. Paul was obviously well aware of the passivity of their antagonist.

"It will be the first time I've done anything like that."

"It's about time, then. Lure him up to your room, say you must slip into something more comfortable. . . ."

Did Paul really mean for her to carry out this ridiculous scenario of a seduction out of a 1940s comedy? Was he luring her into making a fool of herself? Surely the serious Matsushita would be irritated by such ploys, contemptuous of such frivolity. Yet it was decreed that she trust Paul. They were forming an alliance, readying her for combat. Looking innocent, Paul greedily chose a thick wedge of Black Forest cake from the dessert cart.

"You're revealing your age," she teased.

She knew she had passed the test, absorbed his first lesson. Such an image, Judith in a Claudette Colbert negligee, would be vulgar only if it were taken literally. With full concentration and obvious relish, Paul attacked his whipped cream and cherries. He looked up for a moment, his eyes staring coldly into hers.

"Seize life. Manipulate. Invite him up to your room!"

His tone was that of a stern teacher addressing an inexperienced, recalcitrant pupil.

"There is much to be had from this relationship."

She listened. A sophisticated man like Paul must have perceived at once that she hadn't been living, despite all her accomplishments, piled high like a heap of Christmas presents awaiting their recipient; she a writer, a professor, gold stars pinned on her grammar-school compositions, always at the head of the class. But so much time had gone by. How could she know if she were capable of taking such a plunge, suddenly, dramatically, breaking through? Yet it wouldn't do to confess to her real doubts. Paul would find self-pity as unattractive as jealousy. Certainly she couldn't admit how inferior and ill-bred she felt before the high-born Matsushita.

Placing a cigarette in his lapis lazuli holder, Paul leaned forward and offered his final encouragement, paraphrasing Shaw: "One man is as good as another."

Perhaps he had elected to be her teacher, her *sensei*, because he envied her courage at having chosen to believe in the uniqueness of Matsushita.

The next day she telephoned Matsushita's office and left a message that she must speak to him urgently. Matsushita returned the call: "You said 'Urgent.' " She told him she needed photographs of Kuronuma's new film.

Could he bring them to her? Ten-thirty was the only hour possible, Matsushita replied. He would come directly to her room.

Paul had been clairvoyant. Everything seemed possible.

Matsushita arrived at eleven. Under his arm he carried a black zippered case and a family photograph album, filled with dozens of snapshots taken on the set of Kuronuma's film. Looking like an odd couple, the tall Kuronuma and a tiny Matsushita stood side by side in the snow wearing identical cossack caps and ankle-length coats with fur collars, like those favored by Stalin. In one picture Kuronuma and Matsushita sat on the edge of a swimming pool at a Baltic resort. The corners of Kuronuma's lips were turned balefully down. His eyes were woeful, his body slender but flabby, his head octagonally shaped and bald. Matsushita's hair was curled all around his head as if he had affected a woman's poodle cut of the 1950s, so that at first she did not recognize him. His arms were deeply veined and muscular, his belly taut and without a fold of flab. His eyes were liquid and veiled, his face as deeply lined as a jigsaw puzzle. Yet he was expressionless. From the picture it was impossible to guess Matsushita's feelings, to know whether there was harmony or dissension between himself and the notoriously difficult Kuronuma.

Matsushita settled himself in a silk brocade chair. His old weariness reasserted itself. She welcomed this mood which before had accompanied his confessions.

"My father ran a left-wing theater in the thirties," said Matsushita. "He kept it going until it was closed down by the militarists. From then on he did nothing, just sat around the house all day. I couldn't respect him, I hated him. One day he disappeared and the next thing we knew he had moved to Manchuria. He lived there with his mistress until he died."

Matsushita's father had earned the contempt of his son. Yet thirty-five years later this son would attach himself to Kuronuma, aloof, self-absorbed, no more paternal than Matsushita's real father. So her friend was reenacting the rejection of his childhood.

Although his tone remained flat, as if everything that happened to him was beyond repair, he seemed so much in pain that she decided not to point out the obvious connection between Matsushita's past and present. It was he who returned the figure of Kuronuma to their attention.

"*Song of Siberia* will be my last film with him. Then he will have to manage alone. He's impossible."

Matsushita leaned forward. "He expects me to make many trips back and forth to Japan by railroad just to visit his wife and see if she's all right. He'll never call her himself. He's too afraid of her even to telephone. She's a horrible woman, it's true." The image of Kuronuma's wife rose before them: a nagging, shrewish woman, a devourer of the creative force of men. Matsushita was doubly afflicted to be forced to deal with both of them. He warmed to his subject.

"Did you know that during the shooting of his last film he actually slapped the face of an actor in front of everybody? The cameras were rolling. He was talking, just talking. Kuronuma walked over and slapped him hard across the face. Then he didn't like the Russian script girl. He sent me back to Japan to talk a Japanese script girl he knew for many years into coming back to Siberia with me. Of course she refused. I had to beg her, assure her this would be the last time."

And then, with contemptuous irritation, he passed

final judgment on his mentor, the man to whose work he was still exclusively devoting his own efforts. "Kuronuma is a baby!"

Playfully, laughing, as if to dispel the seriousness with which he had outlined Kuronuma's transgressions, he added, "Kuronuma means black swamp!"

With the speed of a storm cloud the old mood returned. Matsushita ran his fingers through his glossy black hair. She wanted to comfort him. The instances of Kuronuma's selfishness were endless. He was seeking her sympathy. She must pull him through this morass, the typically Japanese rationalization of "isn't life hopeless, but it can't, after all, be helped." (*Shikata ga nai.*)

She would infuse him with energy. He was so acutely acquainted with the ways of the world. All he needed was a push, someone who believed in him, who would see him through.

"Become a director yourself," she urged. "Make your own films. Stop sacrificing yourself to Kuronuma. It isn't fair."

All solemnity, as if he were taking her words deeply to heart, Matsushita assumed an aura of unshakable conviction. "I will."

Something important seemed to have been settled between them, all the necessary words spoken. Matushita looked fondly at Judith. "I'll always appreciate your interest," he said.

Then his mood changed again.

"I am old," he sighed. Yet only moments before he seemed confident he might fulfill his creative potential if only he could rid himself of the dead weight of Kuronuma. She sensed that he was comparing himself unfavorably with members of his own generation, men like

Koshima, who had received international recognition despite the increasing commercialization of the Japanese film industry.

"Are you very busy?" Matsushita changed the subject. "If I don't have to return to Siberia, we can spend next week together. I don't have any work to do."

Now that he was offering himself to her, she grew calm, sated. The tension dissipated. She took his overture for granted and even wondered how suddenly it seemed both her due and less worth the having. There was no excitement in their being together, although she wouldn't mind spending some days with him. In any case it seemed again that there was time, no need to rush things. She never saw him as less desirable as when he was accepting her at last.

"I have some appointments," she hedged, "but also a lot of spare time."

Matsushita extended his hand. It was good that they were crossing the chasm of their differences. It also seemed neutral, curiously barren of emotion or joy. Here was Matsushita and yet pleasure seemed ever more distant, receding at the end of a long tunnel. She was talking in her room late at night with a pleasant man exhausted by his long day's work, a casual, nice friend but not one who particularly evoked excitement, the tremors of gypsy violins. At one point Matsushita, gesturing in the luxuriant room, asked, "Do you need all this? My apartment will be empty while I'm away. Perhaps you could wait for me."

She replied matter-of-factly and without particular regret that she had to go home in two weeks to write her book. But they would meet again. "I'll come back," she said. It was she who didn't really care.

Wearing a black turtleneck blouse and paisley pants a

few years out of fashion, she reclined on the bed. There Matsushita joined her, reaching out with so silly a grin on his face that he seemed a naughty child grabbing for the forbidden breasts of its mother. He seemed transformed before her eyes with his soft smile. Was he able to approach her only because he sensed that the pressure was off, that she not only didn't need him, but didn't even want him particularly?

By his manner and the quickness of his motions, he signaled that they were to undress as discreetly as possible. To stare—to admire—was silently pronounced vulgar. When they had settled beside each other, Matsushita became transformed yet again. Like a double-jointed acrobat, agile and with boundless exuberance, he attached himself to her. And so he began, kissing, licking, and sucking at her from every geometrically possible angle, reaching into every part of her body from seemingly impossible directions as if he were a many-tentacled creature of the sea. So swiftly did he move, so deftly and deeply did he penetrate, that Judith could do no more than give herself up completely to his play. His mouth immersed, he lapped and licked, sucked and fondled. He seemed able to go on for hours. Nor would he cease even when she finally cried out for him to stop. With a laugh he went on squeezing and licking until he finally exhausted himself.

This Matsushita was definitely less attractive, less sexual than the man who had held his distance.

After a long while she realized that this multitudinous foreplay was to be all there was, an end in itself, not a prelude to Matsushita entering her with tenderness or otherwise. When she gave him to know she was ready for what was to come next, he grinned and resumed pursuing

her with his tongue. Then, lying back at last, he whispered, first in Japanese, and then in English, "I love you,
I'll love you forever." She wanted it all to mean something, it had to. She forced herself to remember what she
had made of him, his significance, so that even *these* words
undermined it, made their connection finite, too concrete.
The beauty of their relation was supposed to lie in the
number of things they shared the consciousness of not
voicing. Sated with understanding, they should have no
need of superfluous words.

When Matsushita began to lick and kiss her again,
she reached out to touch him. But her hand came up
empty. Naked under the covers, attached to her body like
some sucking mammal, Matsushita contrived to place himself so that she could never once touch, let alone see, his
penis. Able to predict her every move, obviously no
stranger to the rigors of sexual experience, he managed to
remain apart. He seemed perpetually to be moving to the
outer periphery of the bed to avoid her touch. His body
conveyed ambivalence, as if he had once lived entirely for
the senses, submitting to the imperatives of the body, but
had since chosen an ascetic way of life. No caress she had
offered came as a surprise, and she had been permitted to
touch only his head, his face, his arms, and his back. Matsushita's lovemaking was ardent, but full of empty places,
unavowed pockets of boredom—or insecurity—for which
he must have been compensating by this one-sided out-
pouring. And the more he touched her, the more she was
conscious of all the uninhabited parts of himself which
were left untouched. Being with Matsushita was like participating in a ballet in which there was only one dancer—
him. Throughout all was as antiseptic as a hospital. She
was conscious even of longing for the taste of sperm that

would leave the tip of her tongue burning, for some scent, however bitter.

A sly smile remained on his face throughout the night. It was a relief when he finally drifted off. At last she, too, slept. It seemed only seconds before she opened her eyes to discover him above her, his mischievous smile having returned. She wanted to sleep now and there he was, as if compelled to perform. Could he approach her only when she was certain to be no longer capable of being aroused?

Eight or nine short, rapid, uncertain, sporadic thrusts and it was over, the act of a schoolboy his first time out, hardly a reflection of the experienced Matsushita she had imagined. She barely felt his penis at all. As he moved, his strokes seemed unaligned, as if they were coming not from the body of a man who enjoyed being inside a woman, but from somewhere beyond. His body emitted no scent; she had no orgasm; Matsushita seemed neither aware of this nor unaware. The sexual act had been a coda, an amusing little exercise, an afterthought to his performance of the night before. Too delicate to raise the issue of contraception (one could not imagine Matsushita speaking such words), yet too cautious to leave the matter in anyone else's hands, he had sneakily supplied his own device, surreptitiously provided, as if, indeed, he were the sole participant.

By six Matsushita was on his way to the bathroom, still managing to conceal his penis from view, like some Victorian wife whose husband had to be content with what he could make out of her contours in the dark. She didn't hear the toilet flush, if it did. Almost at once Matsushita emerged, neatly dressed. Under his arm he carried the photograph album of snapshots of himself and Kuronuma and his black zippered case which contained an enormous hairbrush.

She sat up in bed.

"Go back to sleep," Matsushita said gently.

"I won't be able to sleep if you go."

"So you are a baby!" he said sharply in a tone that chilled her, for this was what he had called Kuronuma, his tormentor. Morning had brought another Matsushita, one harried and under the mantle of maturity, a man who felt oppressed at having always to pander to the irrational moods of others.

Then he seemed to regret having been so abrupt. "Shall I see you tonight?"

How infuriating that of all nights on this one she had been invited to a screening at the studio of Japan's most brilliant satirical filmmaker. Yet this might be her last chance to see Matsushita. A gnawing doubt had accompanied the morning: Matsushita might very well be summoned back to Siberia by Kuronuma.

She mentioned the name of the director. Matsushita emitted no reaction. Was her innocent reference to this accomplished filmmaker a bitter reminder of his own unfulfilled potential?

"Can you meet me at his studio?" she ventured, even though she knew that Matsushita's presence there would violate protocol. Matsushita belonged to the "Kuronuma group," which rested on laurels of thirty years' duration. For Matsushita to appear at a younger director's studio was tantamount to offering that individual Kuronuma's endorsement.

"I can't do that." His voice trailed off. "I can meet you somewhere else."

She suggested the elevated train station, the only

landmark in this deserted, villagelike pocket of Tokyo, several stops beyond Shinjuku Station. Matsushita agreed, looking vague. She wondered whether he understood her, whether he would be able to find the place. She repeated the directions. He nodded.

Then, suddenly, he added, "I am not worth it. I don't want to ruin your future." He stood there looking at her, after these unusually emphatic words. Then the moment passed. They agreed once more to meet that night. Matsushita said that he might still have to leave for Siberia. Interpreting this as his request that she repledge her interest she said, "Stay!" It seemed as if this was what he wanted; she was certain that he could postpone Siberia and that he wanted to. Kuronuma's whims were something he must have learned to parry, or how could he have provided himself with any personal space at all?

Matsushita departed. Judith dressed and ate breakfast in the hotel coffee shop. For the first time since that panel discussion in Kyoto she felt at home in Japan. She was now truly part of the life here. She would always be *gaijin*, a foreigner, but now she was also someone who belonged. Her tie to Japan was her union with Matsushita. It was not yet complete, but there was plenty of time to refine their relation. She would be accepted here now. For if Matsushita loved her, she could enter at least one of the closed circles of Japanese life from which most foreigners were forever excluded. Sitting in the coffee shop of a Western-style hotel having juice, eggs, toast, and coffee, she felt for the first time how she loved Japan, how exquisite a culture it was, and how lucky she had been to have had the chance to come here.

She went on to the day's screenings, although it took considerable effort for her to pay attention to the films.

Her mind was on the evening when, her work cast aside at last, she could be with Matsushita again. The films concluded. As she was leaving, a secretary handed her a message. Matsushita had called her. How had he known where she would be? Yet he had. Apprehensively she dialed his number.

"I leave for Siberia in the morning," Matsushita announced, the coldness of his voice asserting that she had no leverage. Would he have bothered to phone at all if they had not made an appointment? It was not in his style to leave someone stranded on a street corner, an act which would have rendered him vulnerable to negative judgment by their mutual friends. "I won't be able to see you."

Unable to help herself, desperate, she persisted. "I could cancel my appointments for this evening."

"No," said Matsushita, "it's not possible." Abruptly, he concluded the conversation. "I'm in conference and can't talk anymore."

She replaced the receiver in a pathetic attempt to make it seem as if she were hanging up on him.

Swept now into a cyclone of pain, she was incapable of concealing her tears before secretaries, interpreters, casual passersby. She recalled the odors of her body the night before. Just as Japanese in the nineteenth century had vomited at the smell of butter, Matsushita must have found her repulsive. He was so clean, his hairless, odorless body immaculate. Was it some pungent smell which had repelled him?

At six in the evening, she telephoned his office, determined to restore contact no matter how cruel he might be. He came to the phone.

"I'm so sorry I was rude to you this morning," she said. "That was unforgivable. But I was so upset."

She couldn't go further, admit that her entire world

seemed to be caving in, let alone demand to know what she had done wrong, why he was rejecting her so brutally.

"You must not get into the habit of hanging up like that." He laughed. He forgave her but not to the extent of participating in her distress. He could be soft and playful but not consoling. He would stop well short of emotional commitment. She could almost see his playful smile.

"I'll always remember you," he said. "I'll write to you."

With this she had to be content.

Chapter Four

*T*wo weeks after Matsushita's sudden departure for Siberia, Judith returned to America. Six weeks passed with no word, during which she forced herself to finish her book. Then she wrote an angry letter full of pain to Matsushita's Tokyo address. "I'm asking nothing of you," it began. But a week later she received a letter from Siberia, so long in coming because it must have been read by rival governments and then passed along as being of no political relevance.

In a feeble scrawl, tentative and feminine, the hand of someone wounded, Matsushita apologized. "I am so sorry for the delay in answering to you. Since I was forced to leave you in Tokyo and I left Japan, I was always thinking of you. Our sudden parting gave me the sorrow of missing you. But it is 'c'est la vie' anyhow. I think it should be difficult to express my feeling in a foreign language (English), but I'll try to write you often." What followed was an account of the weather in Siberia ("40 degrees under zero!"), and Matsushita's closing, "with love."

How much more he could have written had he not been confined to English! But it wouldn't be Matsushita's way to write in Japanese, forcing Judith to find someone else, a third party, to translate. He hadn't thought to write in French which she could read, although his conversation had always been sprinkled with French phrases. And wasn't French the language best suited to express his ennui and weariness with the things of this world?

He didn't suggest a time when they could meet again. Judith reasoned that he couldn't have since this would have obliged him to pay her way, and although he moved freely about the world on behalf of Kuronuma, he obviously had no money of his own. She hoped he wouldn't misunderstand her angry letter. But he must surely be as aware as she that any verbal medium was impossible for them.

Matsushita never wrote to her again. After a while, with nowhere to turn, she wrote a bleak, soggy letter to Paul Meredith, reporting on what she called the "Matsushita fiasco." In only one respect was she less than open. She couldn't admit that she and Matsushita had actually spent only one night together, for out of such a meager acquaintance no rational person could possibly build so much. Paul would lose his good opinion of her. She left the number of their encounters vague, and told herself there were times when once was sufficient.

She expected commiseration, but Paul surprised her with a series of letters reporting on actual conversations he had begun to have with Matsushita about her. Matsushita then hadn't forgotten her. It was only that he felt more at ease communicating through Paul. Her old friend had registered the pain in her letter and was determined not to leave her hanging. Paul would take responsibility, draw Matsushita back to her. If Matsushita were receding out of fear, Paul would give him courage.

She thought of Paul Meredith now only with gratitude. Since that day when he had urged her to seize the moment, he had stood with her in her hopes for Matsushita. The intimacy she had finally managed had been owing to him. Now his letters meant that, uncharacteristically, he was taking a stand. He would bolster her spirits, win Matsushita for her where she could not accomplish this alone. She was convinced that Paul was only perverse and destructive with people he didn't like. He is different with me, she concluded.

And she loved this new friendship. Paul was warm and loving, sensitive to Japan and accepted, yet still, like herself, a foreigner. She pushed aside all remaining doubts. Was Paul exaggerating his role? Wasn't it extremely unlikely that Matsushita, with his ancient and noble lineage, should choose a foreigner as his go-between? But Judith was an unlikely choice herself. Matsushita must need her because she awakened in him a desire to go beyond himself, to transcend the barrier between stranger and ally, foreigner and Japanese.

All through the winter Paul revealed a new side of himself, patient and supportive, never condescending, sternly urging faith in herself upon her. Never had a friend so bombarded her with so steady a stream of letters. Each provided as its *pièce de résistance* a conversation with Matsushita in which Paul had managed to insinuate Judith's name. They took place at coffee shops, the locations precisely defined, in Matsushita's office, at the theater, at screenings. Paul made it clear to her that he never asked Matsushita outright whether she should return to Japan; that, he wrote, would be crude and inelegant, most un-Japanese. Instead he would hint and tease. He would drop her name and judge the result.

In one of these letters Paul wrote: "While not in love,

he is very fond. Love is meaningless to him because he does not need it, nor need to feel it. Everything, all his emotion, goes into his work. It is through work that he has chosen to define himself. The work takes all. Completely self-sufficient, he needs nothing more."

Was Paul right? No, this was only the outward Matsushita, the face he permitted outsiders like Paul to see. Matsushita, with his ambiguous smiles, long slender hands, and artist's sensibility, was no insensitive businessman mired in the stultifying intricacies of office politics. How could anyone describe Matsushita as one of those soldiers of the corporation vowing to serve "to the utmost of his ability" (*dor yoku*). Paul was talking about himself, a person who evaded permanent relationships and who thought love was an illusion.

The same letter went on: "The word to describe your relation [Judith blushed as she read, they had discussed her so openly] is *karui*, which means 'light' in the sense of cool, objective, sane. Not detached, but light. This is what, I think, he aspires to. At any rate it is the opposite of hot and heavy. Not that the latter really has any charm for you. You yourself are cool and collected, and in that sense, light. And you like yourself best when you are that way."

Here was Paul being disingenuous, knowing full well how prone she was to the hot and heavy. Was he being sarcastic? Or was he being kind in so persistently defining her by what he believed she *could* be rather than what she was? Maybe he didn't know her as well as she thought he did. They had known each other only in Japan. He knew nothing of Matsushita's predecessors. Nor would he care, because his policy was to take people for what they were at the moment—as if to inspire them to become their best selves. This was one of Paul's most attractive qualities. It had allowed her to feel safe with him, as with almost no one else.

Paul had concluded: "At any rate, so far as guidelines are possible, this might be one of them. If you are tempted to interpret this as dampening, you are dumb, or I am explaining things badly."

Her spirits had in fact been dampened. *Karui* meant sane, but also uncommitted; detached was sister to disinterested. She didn't allow herself to despair, because the image of Paul stood before her. He would be disappointed if she were so greedy as to be dissatisfied with this much bounty. Paul would see that she would be cool and collected. She had a choice.

Paul saw Matsushita often during these months because suddenly, felicitously, they had become involved together in a film project. As soon as it happened, Paul wrote her of this good news:

"I was having lunch with Matsushita yesterday. He spoke of you most affectionately, as indeed did I. Then he brought forth the surprise. He and Kuronuma wanted me to create and edit and direct a film about Kuronuma. I could have all I wanted from any film, plus all of K's photos, and could ask for anything to be put on film. I mumbled that I was honored, wondering how many years this would take. Then he announced that since he wanted this to coincide on Japanese TV with the opening of the new picture, he had gotten TV time, an hour and a half on May 17th, just two months away.

"To appreciate my dilemma you must realize that I am now in nightly rehearsals for my plays, that I am also editing two books at present, and there is my novel. Yet, accept I did. I wonder if I can do it. I will be a stretcher case come May seventeenth, I think. Well, I always said I was happiest working."

Seeing Matsushita this much, Paul would learn what was in his heart, where *karui* might give way to desire. Yet the film about Kuronuma did not go smoothly, and she wondered how this boded for her reunion with Matsushita.

"I've sure bit off more than I can chew with this film," Paul despaired. "I'm not going to make any May seventeenth deadline. I know that now. He doesn't. He'll get the happy news on the tenth when I see him. Hope he is philosophically inclined. Also, they have not yet agreed to my terms—ten percent of the budget in cash and ten percent of the gross take around the world. We will see."

The news grew more grim:

"Tomorrow dubbing and mixing the K. film," Paul reported. "So it is almost done. It is not what I wanted, but is not all that bad either, though very simple. The exigencies of TV are terrible, so are the exigencies of Nippon, which would not, eventually, allow more than three minutes from any film. While my theme was K.'s never compromising and consequently making something worthwhile, I was compromising daily. Still, all things considered, like making an hour-and-a-half film in a month—it is not that bad. I have a few grayer hairs now but not yet, I think, an ulcer."

What disturbed her most was that Matsushita, having enlisted Paul in the project, now seemed to have abandoned him, evading, not keeping his promises, inaccessible when Paul needed him on practical matters:

"M. was not here for any of it. Went back to USSR and will remain there until both he and K. come back together. M. has his hands so full with all his projects and all that I should not really blame him, but at the same time, goddamn it, when I give a promise to someone that I will get this material or that, I keep it. I didn't get anything from Russia I really needed. He pleads busy-ness which is all very well but I don't think I will work with him again. It is too precarious."

Despite Matsushita's role as producer, Paul was left entirely on his own to see himself through. And so he did:

"Well, the TV show is aired and over. It wasn't so bad, though it was not what I wanted. It had a lot of in-direction in it and I liked that, but I think the Japanese were fairly baffled—as they would be in this land of Hard Sell. Certainly Japanese TV had never seen anything this gratuitous before. I saw Matsushita quite by accident at Harajuku just as he was coming back from the airport. He looked harried but pleased. Not a word from any of them after my TV effort was disclosed."

She wrote to Paul doubting whether she should come back, still waiting for some sign from Matsushita. She decided not to allow his behavior with Paul on the TV film to influence how she felt; she wasn't there; Paul could be difficult and evasive himself; she was hearing only one side. Matsushita still hadn't written, but Paul insisted that it didn't matter. And, once, Paul had spelled out his fears to Matsushita. "Will you run away from her because she is strong, too strong?" "No," Matsushita had replied, "I won't."

His last letter before her departure was entirely en-couraging. "What you have," he wrote, "you very much already have—no answers to letters or not. What you have already is here waiting for you. He would like very much to see you."

She memorized these words. Paul now suggested that

she return right after the Tokyo opening of *Song of Siberia*. Before that Matsushita was certain to be very busy.

Still, nagging doubts persisted. If Matsushita really did wish to see her, why didn't he bestow upon her the gift of inviting her to the gala opening itself. And Paul himself also periodically included doubts about Matsushita's accessibility. "He so habitually holds people at a distance, is so determined on the distant but cordial relationship, so obviously avoids what he would call emotional entanglements, that I was surprised he had come so far with you. But, still, I thought, old dogs learn new tricks; there is hope for us all."

Her plans made, she gave herself up to romantic fantasies. She and Matsushita would drive out of grimy Tokyo in Matsushita's white car, stopping at a deserted hot springs in the mountains. They would alight at a lonely inn. Dressed in identical kimonos, they would pad along the wooden floors of narrow hallways to bathe together, as Japanese lovers were wont to do. Naked together, there would be complete harmony between them, no truth of which they were afraid. Expressions of vulnerability would enhance Matsushita's charm.

They would return to their room where a middle-aged woman in subdued kimono would serve them pale delicacies on small blue-and-white porcelain plates more than a century old. A beautiful woman of indeterminate age, a skilled practitioner of an ancient art, would play the samisen.

Then, beneath the *futon*, their lovemaking this time would require no foreplay, only the coming together of their bodies so that Matsushita's penis would swell to such a size that he would completely fill her up. They would not speak. He would not smile his Cheshire-cat smile in the dark. And within his arms she would lose all consciousness of who she was or what she had been.

Hadn't Matsushita signed his letter, "with love"? Wasn't this a portent of closeness to come?

She chose to be encouraged even by Paul's ambiguities. "As for knowing what it all means," he speculated in one of his last letters, "and where it all stands, well, you are barking up the wrong country. You will NEVER know. So be content with that."

Part
Three

Chapter One

*T*en months since she had last seen Matsushita, Judith disembarked at Haneda Airport. It was once again August. She wore a black pants suit, the jacket pulling tightly across her chest, her shirt sticky. Chosen to make her seem slim, it was clearly a mistake and she felt more self-conscious than usual.

She moved along through customs, speaking to no one, not even to the other uneasy foreigners in line beside her, unbuttoning her jacket in the hope that she might appear less large. In the arrivals room she glanced idly around for Paul, although she knew he would use the opportunity of not coming to demonstrate the limitations of their friendship. He would leave her to fend for herself because it was "good for her." She must never forget that Paul would always flee from doing what was expected of him. Giving up the pretense of believing that she needed him to meet her, weighed down by bulky luggage, a bag in each hand, she staggered across the room toward the door.

An interesting-looking man with a craggy face and well-defined features stared suddenly at her from the corner of the room, about fifteen feet away. He wore a rumpled yellow polo shirt and baggy pants. The expression on his worn face was anguished, harassed, and intent upon something. He didn't seem to be looking for anyone in particular, and yet his eyes were directed toward her.

Stared at so insistently, with such unjustified familiarity, she drew her face up in an angry grimace. She couldn't resist making a show of her disapproval of such xenophobic treatment by turning violently away.

In a twinkling the man slipped outside and disappeared.

Only then was Judith seized by panic. Had the man been Matsushita come to meet her after all? Paul knew her arrival time; Matsushita could easily have found it out from him. Abandoning her suitcase, she rushed outside the arrivals terminal and into the parking lot to search for him, let him know how happy she was to see him. But he had vanished. Convinced that it was Matsushita, she was elated that he had cared enough to come to the airport. Disoriented, she allowed herself to be driven into downtown Tokyo by an illegal gypsy cab driver who charged double the official rate. Her only concern was speed. No doubt Matsushita had decided to proceed directly to her hotel where he would be waiting in the lobby to surprise her.

But when she reached the Ginza Dai-Ichi, a high-rise hotel, simultaneously sleazy and clean, unabashedly glittering and profoundly middle-class, Matsushita was nowhere to be found. Before she even bathed or removed her stale clothes, she dialed his number. Could he have arrived home this rapidly? But he was a fast, frenetic driver, given to sudden, unexpected bursts of speed.

The telephone rang five times before it was picked up. She drew in her breath. A muffled, terse voice, barely audible, replied first in Japanese and then, quickly, in English. It was a voice as frigid as the Siberian winter. "Then you have arrived?"

Matsushita wouldn't acknowledge that he had been at the airport. Nor did she ask if he had been there. How could she admit that she didn't recognize the person she had traveled ten thousand miles to see? Matsushita followed with a series of short questions, all impersonal, all correct.

"Where are you staying?" "How long are you staying?" "Have you come to work?" It was as if she were talking to a stranger.

Yet it was exhilarating to be in contact with Matsushita again, despite his impersonality. Of course he would be angry with her for not having recognized him at the airport. Her punishment was this frigid welcome, the coldest tones Matsushita had ever adopted since she had known him.

She plunged onward. "When can I see you?" and then, quickly, "Can I see you tonight?"

"Not tonight," Matsushita said evasively. "I have a conference about a new film project at ten in the morning. People will begin gathering in my office at ten," he repeated, polite but definite. "Ring me up at one o'clock tomorrow afternoon. I'll know my schedule better then. Good night."

Judith barely had the opportunity to echo her good night when he replaced the receiver.

Now it seemed that by not recognizing Matsushita at the airport she had ruined everything. She sat without moving in the tiny cell-like room—bed, chest of drawers, television, one window. She willed herself not to feel anything, to be so numb that she wouldn't register Matsushita's coldness. The sheets on the narrow bed were

dotted with cigarette burns. On television a program fea-
tured three former Japanese Olympic medalists. A mara-
thon runner had once placed third. Four years later he left
a suicide note explaining that he was "thoroughly exhausted." Failure demanded nothing less than annihilation
of the self. A boxer who had won a gold medal was pic-
tured in the snack bar he subsequently opened.

Despite her weariness, sleep did not come easily that
night. She lay in bed and told herself that panic would
only confirm defeat. Her misunderstanding with Matsushita was trivial; it could be overcome. Once she gained
entry to him, she would reawaken his need. For who else
could offer him so safe a refuge, with whom else could he
unburden himself? His creativity had long been stifled by
the formalities of his role as producer for Kuronuma in
this land rigid with hierarchies. She would release him.
He would show gratitude, affection.

All morning as she waited in her room, she was calm,
confident that her mistake could be rectified. At one she
dialed. A secretary answered.

"Mr. Matsushita is not here." She pronounced the
words so automatically and so purposefully that they
seemed to have been rehearsed. "You are invited to come
to his office at five-thirty with Paul Meredith. Mr. Matsushita has another appointment at seven-thirty."

So a group encounter had already been carefully arranged to create the maximum distance.

Still she wouldn't permit herself to draw irrevocable
conclusions. The Matsushita she had known had a pliant,
easygoing side. He was self-effacing. Never had he been
so full of his own importance as to be pretentious. She
would get through to him.

If she had been alone, she would have been terrified before the difficulty of finding Matsushita's office. Houses in Tokyo were often unmarked or numbered according to when the building was constructed rather than by its numerical relation to the others on the street. This time, in any case, it was simple because Matsushita had set himself up in a suite of rooms in a central if unfashionable hotel not far from the Ginza.

Paul did not reveal what he was thinking as they walked to Matsushita's office. He eased himself into the role of innocent bystander. Perhaps he hoped that his presence alone would make a difference. This was the Japanese way. Whenever he could, Paul acceded to it. His every gesture refused to acknowledge that she might break down at any moment.

The floor on which Matsushita's office was located was deserted. The doors bore no identifying names so that it was impossible to determine what kind of business was being conducted here. At the end of the hall they stopped.

Suddenly in a room that had seemed empty, a flock of young women fluttered to their side. They were nondescript, not at all pretty, and acted as if they were teachers of the art of politeness. Their smiles conveyed that they were eager to please, while a certain distance let it be known that their cordiality was at the service of an appointed end. Their white blouses and dark skirts above their knees made them seem like superannuated schoolgirls.

Judith and Paul were ushered at once into Matsushita's office. It was a large room neatly decorated with matching white leather couches and armchairs that looked as if they had just been unpacked. On Matsushita's long rectangular desk were three white ultramodern push-button telephones. Not a stray paper clip interrupted its surface of polished wood. This was clearly the office of a very important, if newly arrived, executive.

Matsushita bounded into the room with coy little bobbings of his head. Toward Judith he made a vague gesture, his arms stretched out. He pointed to her presence, but no more. Their eyes glanced past each other. Matsushita didn't seem to notice when she looked away.

It was Matsushita who was to be the star of the occasion, enjoying all the ensuing prerogatives. He wore a white Cardin jumpsuit, a style now popular in Japan among men in their early twenties, half Matsushita's age. An outrageous bright orange shirt of some silky material peeped out to complete the outfit. She couldn't take her eyes off that skin-tight jumpsuit. Matsushita looked like a continental Barbie doll, not Barbie's cleancut American mate, Ken, but a more exotic rival.

Matsushita motioned for Paul and Judith to be seated on the couch while he drew up a chair in front of them. One of the secretaries entered carrying tiny cups of very strong coffee, a predictable and correct, if paltry token of his hospitality. There was no *yōkan*, that sweet bean gelatin whose rich sweetness belied its unpleasing physical resemblance to brown aspic. With such a distraction Judith could have preoccupied herself, the sweetness pushing down the pain, postponing her having to deal with this new Matsushita. But nothing festive marked the meeting, no tea with cherry-blossom petals floating on its surface. Matsushita was either determined to avoid or incapable of offering gratuitous gestures of good will.

Matsushita's distance brought Judith and Paul together. As if by telepathy they agreed not to touch the coffee. Judith moved from the couch to one of the armchairs so that, as Matsushita addressed himself to Paul, he couldn't include her in the business of the day. He no longer had the task of acknowledging her presence with those ventriloquistlike nods which he assumed fell within the limits of cordiality.

The purpose of the meeting, Matsushita now revealed, was that he wished to invite Paul formally to make a theatrical documentary film about Kuronuma. The television film had created a stir, winning a prize as one of the best programs of the year, despite the fact that Kuronuma had long been out of fashion.

"I want you to have whatever money you need," this new Matsushita began. The old Matsushita would have conducted himself like one of his samurai ancestors who were tormented after the Meiji Restoration by the necessity of using money, even of doing arithmetic, which they believed vulgar and degrading. Forced to do errands that included handling currency, these samurai would wrap their faces with hand towels and go out only after dark.

Paul made a gesture of assent, but said nothing. At least for him, money was not the issue. Instead, he changed the direction of the conversation in so abrupt a manner that if Matsushita were a man given to telegraphing his reactions through facial expressions he would have appeared to be annoyed or at least startled by what was clearly a rebuke.

"What do you see as the theatrical possibilities for such a film?"

Ignored now by both men, Judith stopped listening. She pondered the transformed Matsushita. It was no wonder that she had not recognized him yesterday, despite what must have been his Sunday mask of vulnerability.

How incongruous the Cardin jumpsuit was with Matsushita's deeply lined face, so much more wrinkled than that of Kuronuma, twenty years his senior. Something else was changed too. She realized now that, as in the snapshots of Matsushita and Kuronuma in Siberia, Matsushita's hair was once again fluffy and curled with a permanent wave in failed defiance of the prematurely lined face. And no longer was it thickly threaded with gray! *"Pāmas"* had become a fad among young Japanese men remaking themselves on the model of the foreign barbarians. And so Matsushita had had his beautiful hair curled with a hot iron in a beauty salon, as Japanese women did after the war. But yesterday the man at the airport hadn't seemed to have the tight black curls of a poodle. Could she have been wrong? But no, if it hadn't been Matsushita at the airport, how was she to account for his hostility when she telephoned? It was more likely that she didn't notice the *pāma* because it was not what she expected; she had seen the Matsushita of her fantasies, the image of months of desire.

The deeply etched lines across his face, snaking up and down its wide contours, made him look, as he always had, perpetually in pain, although he was now gesturing and laughing with Paul. His face still expressed the anguish of someone tormented by a forbidden desire.

Mute, she watched as if she were uninvolved, an outsider surveying a scene which did not particularly concern her, as if what Matsushita said or didn't say, did or didn't do, touched her only as an observer of an interesting stranger. From the dimness in which she sat, she could no longer register the discrepancy between this man now gesturing so fulsomely, an animated if plastic vision in white, and the one who had told Paul that, "Yes, she should indeed come back to Japan. I would be delighted to see her."

Matsushita kept himself within the boundaries of his

pantomime of contempt. He would discuss only how Paul's television documentary could be converted into a 35-millimeter film. Solemnly Matsushita promised Paul that if he agreed to direct this film, it would be entered in all the major film festivals. Judith watched, spellbound, as Matsushita felt his way, searching for a soft spot that would ensure Paul's acquiescence, despite the uncertainties and bitterness of their experience working on the television film.

She could feel Paul hesitating. Did he really wish to turn Matsushita down yet feel unable to do so out of deference to the Japanese manner? Would Paul act on his annoyance at the unkept promises about footage, equipment, and documents that were supposed to have been made available but which never materialized?

These promises to Paul, she knew, had been fabrications spun by Matsushita to meet the exigencies of the moment. It would be bad manners to refer to them today, and so Matsushita could remain secure in his bad faith. Paul had listed all the disappointments which made his work on the television film so frustrating. But maybe he stopped here only because he feared confrontations of any kind.

To Judith he seemed suddenly weary of detailing what could not now be altered. She wondered whether his responses were colored by his consciousness of her sitting numbly by, so still that it appeared she wasn't even breathing. Paul pressed on, but, she thought, his tone, uncertain now, gave him away.

"If we don't come to an agreement, will someone else be asked to do it?"

Matsushita seemed to emit the indiscretion of a long sigh of relief. Paul, the foreigner still, despite his thirty years in this country, had refused even in a business relationship, to conceal his own needs. He would be subject to Matsushita's manipulations because he cared. He wanted to be the voice of Kuronuma. He was vulnerable because making the film mattered to him.

With this question he had afforded Matsushita a glimpse of his anxiety. Exposing his desire to retain his role as interpreter of the work of Kuronuma to the outside, he had forfeited his equality with this new Matsushita. More at ease now than at any moment in the meeting, Matsushita nodded quietly, all calm, all command.

"It will be done, whether by a Japanese or a foreigner."

This was a far cry from the humble, endearingly self-deprecating Matsushita Judith had first met, a man who always seemed sad, his liquid brown eyes defeated, his full sensual mouth with its outermost corners perpetually turned downward. This was not the man who after they had gone to bed together had said, "I am not worth it."

Throughout the winter she had heard Matsushita whispering, "I am not worth it." What could he have meant? Could he childishly have expected her to pour forth protestations, proclaim his sublime value? She took it for granted that he knew his beauty and refinement rendered him obviously worthy of any woman's love.

Or had he simply used these words to separate himself from her?

But she remembered, too, that the closer she and Matsushita had drawn together, the more he made it seem as if he were forced into seeing her—denying this was so with the cliché that if he didn't wish to be with her, then he wouldn't be. Had he heard that line in some American film of his childhood?

For three years he had existed for her as a magnificent artifact, a work of art unearthed whole and untarnished. She'd seen him as a man who made no connection between being potent and bullying. Forced to live in the 1970s, he seemed disoriented, a throwback. Given the unwholesome values of the day, perhaps it was no wonder that he had learned to be ashamed of his body, even keeping his penis hidden from sight during the sexual act.

Yet today marked the unveiling of a man who was not averse to the requirements of setting events in motion. He seemed more ample of face as well as of hairdo, and even fuller of bottom. He was a man she did not know.

She told herself she had only herself to blame for his distance. Paul didn't know what happened at the airport because she had been too ashamed to tell him. Did she even deserve Matsushita if his reality took second place to her fantasies of him?

She stared uneasily around Matsushita's new offices. The neatness and order dared her scrutinizing eyes to discover anything they were not sanctioned to know. Meanwhile Matsushita was growing tentative, suggesting that it was of no real moment to him whether Paul made the film he had suggested. That this contradicted his having arranged the meeting in the first place didn't seem to bother him.

When she had mailed Matsushita a copy of her book, *The Art of Film, East and West*, inscribing "with love" on the inside cover, this gift had gone unacknowledged, although Paul had written that he saw Matsushita at a coffee bar and Matsushita had remarked how well Judith looked in her photograph on the jacket.

"She's very beautiful, isn't she?" he had said with what Paul took to be the pleasure of a proprietary right.

To have written and thanked her, she knew, would have admitted a significance to the giver of the gift in Matsushita's life. Yet one couldn't be sure. Didn't Matsushita always prefer not to transmit his feelings in words, let alone in those of a foreign language which, confined to their ungrammatical utility, couldn't possibly convey his sentiments?

She sat waiting for Paul to conclude this meeting, which seemed interminable because Matsushita kept on interrupting the discussion to take telephone calls. Every five minutes one of his underlings would appear with a paper for him to sign. Had he deliberately arranged this so as to convey to Judith and Paul his new importance?

The hour drew to its close. Paul said that, of course, he felt enormous sympathy for Kuronuma and would be glad to make the film, provided that the terms were acceptable. With a culminating burst of ingratiating charm, Matsushita leaned forward and confided (as if rewarding Paul's amenability by conferring some precious gift), that Kuronuma had bursitis in his knee joints and found it painful to walk. A piece of inside information. Paul murmured appropriate condolences, abiding by the forms to the last.

"Don't disappoint me." Matsushita beamed at Paul, white teeth flashing. They were now standing, about to take their leave. The Cardin jumpsuit, which looked as if it would glow in the dark, made the image of the slight, stooped, shabby man at the airport, his narrow shoulders hunched together, seem almost a hallucination.

Matsushita kept up his performance until the end, never faltering once. Without looking Judith in the eye, he shook her hand and she moved to the door unimpeded. Paul said a few final words and it was over.

Part
Four

Chapter One

*T*he morning after their visit to Matsushita's office, Paul telephoned. As if nothing unusual had happened, he invited her to lunch. In gratitude for his concern, she refrained from referring to her misery. They were to meet in front of the Mitsukoshi department store on Ginza Street. And exactly at the appointed moment Paul sauntered up in white shirt and tie, jaunty tweed sport jacket, and an affectionate smile through which she saw at once that his object today would be to convey that none of this was to be taken terribly seriously, that in fact not much had been lost. It would do no good to accuse him of having misled her; she read him as utterly incapable of taking responsibility for people's failures to do what others wanted them to.

"We're going to one of my favorite places," Paul began, tucking Judith's arm into his, as he led her to a tiny restaurant cater-cornered to two busy streets. The place was called Tenryu, the Heavenly Dragon. At this noon hour it was bustling with customers. Wax models of the specialties of the house gathered dust behind the plate-glass window. Not a single foreigner could be seen within.

Paul, however, breezed right through, leading her up to a little balcony with five tables, from which they could survey the crowd below and yet not be disturbed.

"I'm addicted to these things," said Paul, pointing to the Chinese-style fried dumplings being passed around. And almost as soon as they seated themselves a waiter placed before them two huge plates of them. Enclosed within each was a shiny globule of pork, nearly white with fat. Before a bite could be taken, the entire entity had to be lifted aloft, dipped in hot oil, and carried with a modicum of grace, not to mention cleanliness, to the mouth. There didn't seem to be a fork or knife in the place either, a predictable tactic of the owners to discourage foreign patrons.

Paul smiled maliciously and attacked his dumplings. Judith, delaying as long as possible, stared down at the main room below, filled with Japanese men of all ages and sizes in white shirts and black pants. No one was alone; everyone came in a group, laughing and talking and, it seemed, consciously avoiding so much as a stare at the foreigners above. The usual segregation was in force. Judith was the only woman there.

Paul devoured his dumplings, without so much as a drop of oil or grease descending either to the table or his white shirt. Judith's first effort resulted, as she knew it would, in catastrophe. The slimy dumpling slipped precipitously from the chopsticks onto the plate, joining its companions in victory, splashing in an excess of glee as it splattered oil onto both Judith and Paul indiscriminately. Paul turned away, pretending not to notice what had happened. Was he enjoying her struggle, the inelegance of her manner illuminating why Matsushita had rejected her? What could even the most highly skilled, the most delicate of intermediaries, do with so awkward, so graceless a woman? Yes, he had deliberately brought her here to make precisely this point.

Then it appeared that what Paul was actually doing was casting his eyes on a waiter standing just beyond her chair. The waiter approached to ask if they required anything more. He was a heavyset, rough-looking boy with thick stubby fingers and a fat neck. His skin was dun colored, almost brown, his lips thin and set in a cynical smile, his black hair coarse and standing up in a cowlick.

This boy had eyes only for Paul. The feeling appeared increasingly mutual. She didn't mind Paul's inattention. Her consciousness began to set around the wily shape of Matsushita once more.

Abruptly Paul remembered his social obligation to her.

"When I left you last night I had dinner with some very old friends, a woman with whom I had an affair twenty years ago and her husband," he said.

He had decided to play one of his favorite roles: the catalyst releasing the most feline and surreptitious feelings of others. What could she do but play along?

"Did the husband know?"

"Of course. He behaved quite naturally. At the table the three of us were like a happy family reunited."

"Does the woman still care for you? Was she comparing you the whole time with this husband?"

"Yes, there were the old vibrations. In a sense it was exactly as it was between us twenty years ago. And she looked ravishing. She hadn't aged a day. I still wanted her. But, of course, nothing happened. Our eyes met, our hands brushed lightly against each other. We fanned the embers of old feelings, and the truth is the husband didn't even mind. He may have been proud that I still found his wife attractive. The continuity of the erotic impulse which the Japanese maintain so exquisitely."

Judith sat silent.

"No one ever forgets," Paul concluded. "This continuity of feelings is what keeps me in Japan."

"I wish I could have that with Matsushita," Judith said.

"You have not chosen wisely," Paul stated gently.

The waiter was now staring quite boldly at Paul, clearly interested, without shame. He hovered nearby, waiting for Paul to close the encounter by naming a time and place of rendezvous.

She watched the little drama unfold. A Tokyo hustler would have known precisely how to manipulate so delicious a catch as Paul, miraculously struggling on his hook. This country boy had unnecessarily granted Paul the upper hand. She could feel Paul's delight in the victory. Paul could now reel *him* in, taking a generous slice of his pleasure from control of this husky, muscular prey.

Paul smiled and waited, testing the boy's interest. It was obvious, at least to her, what his signals meant: whatever happened between them, it could not result from anything so vulgar as need on the part of the older man. She saw that this encounter had allowed Paul to cut through the viscosity of her pain. He was now fortified enough to be generous, to offer his solicitude.

"Call him," she begged. "Ask him why he's done this. Tell him I'm leaving tomorrow. Tell him I came to Japan only because he told you he wanted me to. 'Shall we invite her to come back?' Isn't that what he said?" She was appalled that she had actually quoted his own letters back to him.

To her relief he pretended not to notice. Instead he smiled affectionately. "You know it won't do any good."

He was agreeing to call Matsushita. Unless she immediately prevented him, he would assume that task. Could a friend do less?

"After all, I feel somewhat responsible. He used me. I was the sign. And then, obviously, I wasn't. How clever he is. And you, you're such an innocent."

"I know I'm being stupid," she replied, counting on his inclination to acknowledge people their obsessions. It violated Paul's sense of himself to take moral distance from people's personal lives. His style was to set an example of tolerance in the hope that he would be treated in kind.

"No matter how he felt, to be cruel to you, even if out of fear, makes him a lousy person."

She still couldn't admit that Matsushita's behavior was probably inspired by her failure to recognize him at the airport. She desperately wished she could ask Paul about this. Perhaps Matsushita hadn't wanted to be recognized at all. He had hung back and stared at her from the expanse of the arrivals terminal.

"What are your plans now?" Paul pursued. "You're not going to sit in that hotel room, are you?"

"My feelings haven't changed."

She defied Paul to demand that they close the book on Matsushita. Surely it was too early.

Paul gave her a long look. She saw that he would remain for a time in her boat, keep her, if not all her hopes, afloat. She had not been wrong. His mistaken judgment about Matsushita had drawn him to her, like a parent whose child had done itself some injury through the parent's carelessness. But she could also hear his silent self-congratulation. He must be telling himself (if he had ever doubted it) that he was right never to have demanded more in his own relationships than was offered, nor most of the time to offer more than he felt like giving. It was good how Japanese he had become. She was thankful that he would not speak these words.

"I'll call him this afternoon."

The hour was over. The waiters who had been balancing the plates of glossy fried dumplings like circus jugglers had disappeared. The men in white short-sleeved shirts ringed with sweat who had gulped down their greasy lunches without so much as soiling their fingertips had returned to the steel and glass edifices ringing the Ginza.

Paul shifted the subject to more neutral ground as they made their way down the narrow flight of stairs. "In this country it's considered more courageous to conform."

"Rebellion is more interesting," Judith replied, knowing that Paul didn't think so. Like the Japanese, he preferred to live by a narrow set of rules, arbitrary, never to be violated. The only difference was that as a foreigner he could make his own rules, while those of the Japanese were appointed, laid out like fresh clothes superintended by zealous housewives. It was now part of the ritual of their friendship that each time they met they lay out their differences.

Paul ran for the subway. Judith remained on the noisy, hot Ginza. The ravenous self which had transported her back to Japan, the self that could be satisfied only with Matsushita, shook the bars of its confinement once Paul had vanished. By an act of will she dragged herself back to the hotel. There she waited until five, when Paul telephoned to report that he had spoken with Matsushita.

"I had to admit that you came back to Japan just to see him. Then I asked, not pressing too much, whether he shouldn't explain himself. That was it. He said, 'I'll see her,' and we left it at that."

She forced herself to become rigid, to feel nothing and so not be overcome by humiliation. Yet she wanted to submit to the feeling too. The bars of the cage rattled.

She remained in her room that night and the following morning, abandoning her post only for lunch in the coffee shop. When she returned there was a message in her box from Matsushita: "Please come to the Diamond Hotel at twelve-thirty tomorrow." The Diamond was that hotel whose upper floor housed Matsushita's office.

She made ready to give herself over to him, dedicating the next twenty-four hours to reflection as if Matsushita were a book she was reviewing, a film she had to analyze.

In the morning she was calm, choosing from a carelessly packed wardrobe. She would wear a red cotton dress with a long gold zipper snaking up the front. Its straight lines were slimming. She couldn't hope to imitate the Japanese girls parading around the Ginza in tight T-shirts. She was too old, too much of another era.

She had considered bringing Matsushita some gift, an offering, as was the custom when paying calls in Japan. She had thought long about a present that would please him, regardless of cost, something of expensive leather perhaps, with his initials embossed in gold. It would have to be a leather soft as silk, liquid to the touch, an object he would not buy for himself. But then a present had seemed an even greater risk than her return itself. Any selection would have been too definite. What if her choice had been wrong? What if any gift at all would prove an embarrassment? In any case, it was too late now to consider whether some object wrapped and beribboned would have made this lunch easier.

The day was hot and still. The air was again heavy

and motionless, so that one felt grateful for Tokyo's air-conditioned taxis, taken for granted as a requisite of civilized life. The driver had no difficulty locating the Diamond Hotel. The dining room was at street level. She entered to find it completely empty. Languid waiters, their shirts not quite fresh, stood idly about the room. She chose a table and buried herself in the book she had brought. Now that she was here she felt only terror at the prospect of facing Matsushita.

Twenty minutes passed. Finally through her peripheral vision she saw Matsushita rushing through the door. He glided over to the table, choosing to sit not opposite but beside her on the leather bench against the wall.

Today he was not wearing the Cardin jumpsuit. Dressed simply in a white shirt open at the neck and dark trousers, he appeared open and accessible, unassertive in the manner she remembered. As it had in the past, his elegance resided in the face, in that world-weary look of a man who could name a score of ancestors.

Matsushita flashed a smile that, like a streak of lightning, disappeared as rapidly as it came. He asked how she was, clinging to the pleasantries. She knew some time must pass before they could connect. First they would have to circle each other. Slowly they would create a core of understanding. He was with her again at last, even if he had been coerced into attending this meeting.

"Shall we order lunch? Would you like to look at the menu?"

He handed her the fake leather notebook.

"What would you like?"

He pursued this ordering of lunch hurriedly and with great urgency. Obediently she directed her attention to the stained menu. A waiter hovered, unimpressed.

Everything on the menu appeared to be an uneasy, inadequate imitation of a Western dish. Judith waited for Matsushita to order. Then she chose what he did. Their full-course plastic lunch was served instantly.

It was painfully clear that Matsushita was suffering and had come only because he could not refuse Paul. Why else was he so discomfited, impersonal, and removed?

The waiter made minimal attempts to serve them in style, but his careless efforts only pointed up the tawdriness of the occasion. Everything was set on the table at once, rendered even more humiliating by the swipe at ceremony, everything hopelessly in the Western style. There was a slightly wilted salad flowing over the sides of the large soup plate in which it was served. The tough, lukewarm chicken had been reheated. The bread tray contained a substance softer and pastier than Wonder Bread. Garish red and blue plastic flowers manufactured in Hong Kong adorned the table, insulting in their falseness.

Matsushita began to pick his way delicately through his food, seemingly unaware of its character, or indeed of what it was he consumed. Judith now knew beyond doubt that he had chosen this seedy, run-down place not out of convenience, although this, too, was served by his decision, but more particularly to demonstrate that she was of no consequence to him.

There was to be no reunion, no reversal of the performance at his office. Nor was this to be the occasion of a formal explanation at which Matsushita sadly, regretfully, pointed out that his feelings had changed, or that Paul and Judith had misunderstood him, or that his circumstances had altered so that he could no longer be responsible for promises construed from his words to Paul.

Least of all was Matsushita about to admit that he

had been at Haneda Airport and that Judith's own hostility had led him to want nothing more to do with her.

Rather, since she demanded it, she was being treated
to a new Matsushita, one for whom such clarifications
would at best be frivolous. It was a Matsushita too practical to participate in emotional scenes from which no material benefit could accrue.

"Kuronuma-san will be grateful," he said suddenly,
looking at her with a wide, toothy, ingratiating smile.

She was to pay for the trouble she had caused him.
The tally had been figured up and handed to her, like a
spiraling strip of addition torn from a calculator. She was
to serve Matsushita as his messenger. Specifically, she was
to aid him in ensnaring Paul so that he might agree to
make the documentary about Kuronuma. Ironically, Matsushita did not know that she had no leverage with which
to negotiate. Paul would agree no matter what the terms,
if only so that no one else would make the film. If she
wished to play the card of her special relationship with
Paul as a means of keeping the thread of contact with
Matsushita, she must do so at once. Its devaluation was
imminent.

In another culture, Judith reflected, Matsushita
might more clearly be perceived as a gigolo, a person who
openly sold himself for the pleasure of others. Only
Matsushita did not need women at all. A gigolo without
women, he plied his trade among investors, producers,
and functionaries of conglomerates. His methods of per-
suasion were directed not toward winning the approval of
a woman, but toward inducing actors, cinematographers,
and crew members to sign on once more with the difficult
Kuronuma. He enlisted his sensuality without resort to
sex.

It struck her that Matsushita was deploying his erotic charm even now here with her, as if the illusion of passion were the primary asset with which he did business on his particular commodities market. Hadn't Paul once suggested that Matsushita might not be wholly heterosexual? Paul had once mentioned a long homosexual affair which consumed Matsushita while he was in college. And now while Matsushita awaited her answer, some reply that would reveal where Paul stood with regard to the documentary about Kuronuma, she recalled Paul's use of the word *karui*—cold dispassion, the very control she once had found so intriguing.

Delighted with him in her hotel room ten months earlier, she had mourned, "We shall grow old." But insensitive to her desperation to hold on to the perfect moment, Matsushita had replied tensely, "Of course." Was he even then trying to save himself by bringing forth the chilling note of the pragmatic, lest his smooth body and warm smile lead a naïve woman to the wrong conclusion regarding his capacity for commitment? Had he been explaining that the more intense the passion, the more dangerous and debilitating he found it? His eyes, his face, his touch conveyed a silken sensuality, easy entry to a magnificent pasha's den of sexual variety. But hadn't his words always connoted something else?

When, after months of frantic work, Paul's television film about Kuronuma had been aired, Matsushita had never called either to offer him congratulations or to comment on the film in any way. He had never indicated whether he had even seen it. Paul had thought, wrongly as it turned out, that Matsushita had not been in Japan at the time. A month later they had run into each other at a coffee shop and then, as if in passing, Matsushita with a grin had passed on Kuronuma's reaction: " 'He sure packed a lot into seventy minutes.' "

Now Matsushita confidently waited for Judith to tell him what he wished to know of Paul's intentions.

"Since you never even called after Paul made the first film, why should he do a second?"

Matsushita remained impassive. "I was too busy." He added a weary look that begged her to sympathize with him in his dismay at being so harassed.

Kuronuma was so demanding, he seemed to be saying, whereas Matsushita, for all his efforts, never asked anything for himself. He sought only to facilitate the work of others. The least Judith and Paul could do was to nurture him.

At their meeting in Matsushita's office, Paul had protested that although Matsushita took credit as the producer of the television film, he had actually done none of the work himself. He had provided no technical assistance and, worse, he had relegated everything to incompetent underlings. Would this happen again? Paul had asked bluntly. And then Matsushita had produced the identical words he had murmured to Judith during their last night together ten months before. "Next time it will be different."

"I trust you to help me," Matsushita now ventured.

Never had she felt so miserably abject. Now that she was here it didn't seem even to matter that she was with Matsushita. She saw herself as if from the outside looking in, suspended in old feelings. The conversation must be made more personal, it couldn't be confined to that infernal documentary. She must force Matsushita if not to appreciate her, then at least to feel sorry, guilty, unjust. Then the spell would be broken and she could freely resume her life. And yet the proximity of freedom produced a violent reaction, the need to continue to remain caged.

"Were you lying when you told Paul you wanted to see me? Why did you lie?"

"I wasn't lying."

Consistency would have had him acknowledge that he had deceived Paul. Or that he had changed his mind. But what did Matsushita care for consistency or logic, Western encumbrances of "no concern" to him? No, resolutely he would hold to the Japanese way, the intuitive, the oblique, the *non sequitur* which he hoped would be taken for subtlety.

"I want to help you with your work. Anything I can do for you, just let me know. I'll put one of my secretaries at your disposal, from morning to night, for as long as you wish."

When had she ever enlisted Matsushita to facilitate her writing? All he had ever done was provide the photographs of himself and Kuronuma which had served as her pretext to lure him to her hotel room on that night ten months ago. He wished to play the benevolent autocrat kindly assisting the struggling foreign writer.

But she had not returned to Tokyo this time to work. She must dismantle this foundation even as he was setting the bricks neatly in place. Who cared if she had to be blunt!

"I don't need any help."

She wasn't about to let him off so easily. But how to shatter his composure. Let him hate her—hadn't she already suffered the worst? She would insult him, accuse him of base motives. This at last might summon his best self, the old Matsushita, if only to rise in denial.

"Haven't you agreed to see me only because you

hope I'll help you convince Paul to make your movie?"

"I don't care about that," said Matsushita. "I can always get someone else. It doesn't matter to me at all."

This she could no longer doubt, for this new, enterprising Matsushita would certainly find someone to accommodate him. She fell silent, thwarted. She tried to anticipate his strategy. She could feel him readying himself for another effort to close the circle, eliminate any residual ambiguity, even if it meant he had to step out of character and breach decorum by verbalizing his feelings.

"Did you come to Japan just to see me?" His tone was sober and even. No one might accuse him of attempting to humiliate her. But in English he was able to sound only two notes, one of gaiety and joy, obviously of no use to him today, and the other the stiff, businesslike manner in which he did his work.

Acutely conscious of his physical presence, of his capacity for passion now beyond her reach, she was afraid to look at him. When she did, it was to perceive a magnificent piece of sculpture, one without blood, gore, or sticky secretions, a statue one might pause before in a museum. She admired, and not a word they had been saying made any sense.

"I would have done things differently," she evaded, too ashamed and humiliated to tell him the truth. For here in this sleazy dining room what could be more absurd than her feeling for a man who only wanted to be rid of her? She sensed that he was making an effort to stifle his distaste for the vulgarity of unrequited love, the unseemliness, the boredom of it. She felt as if every word she had uttered was a lie because it presumed a connection between them. The reality was that they were virtually total strangers.

"I would like to pay for your accommodations. Let it be a gift from *Song of Siberia* to you."

"I can't accept that. You will do nothing of the kind. I have plenty of money and, in any case, money means nothing to me."

She couldn't even turn to look at him, to read what she knew must be written on his face—exasperated disappointment at her stubborn refusal to do the decorous thing, to recede gracefully and without further confrontation. Matsushita would have to be doubly angered now, for having been forced to speak so openly and in such crass, obvious terms. Miserably she was conscious that no matter what she said or did, all control, all power over the situation remained firmly in his hands.

"When are you leaving?" he asked, as if this would finally convince her of his indifference.

"I wish I could leave this very minute!"

This further outburst of emotion failed to touch him. Probably he interpreted it as her assenting to his view of the reality. She must at last be accepting that he wasn't about to fulfill her expectations.

"Stay," he said, revising the terms of the transaction, inviting her to remain so that there might be a sizable hotel bill for him to pay.

"To what purpose?" Judith asked, determined to pretend that it was still possible to buy time and begin all over again—to struggle for love withheld. The greatest pain imaginable was not the cruel rejection of Matsushita, but the emptiness of not being abused and cast off.

"To talk," Matsushita improvised vaguely. "Paul told me you want a friend in Tokyo." She couldn't decide whether the choice of the word "friend" was a result of his faulty English, now rapidly failing him, or a calculated refusal to acknowledge that love, affection, was the issue. "I have been too busy planning this campaign for Kuronuma-san's new film."

"Why didn't you write?" she demanded, picking up the thread of his assertion that he had not lied. The content of Paul's letters rose before her, and she struggled to make them connect as if they were a failed electric circuit. Frantically she was placing cathodes here, then there, determined at all cost to generate a spark.

"I was too tired to write in English."

Was there some victory here? She wished desperately that Matsushita would accompany this remarkable statement with some gesture of affection, that he might touch her now instead of speaking into the void. Was she to conclude that if she had been able to read Japanese, he might have wooed her with love letters all these many months? But it was too risky to pursue this line of reasoning.

"You wrote so many letters," Matsushita murmured, as if in wonder that anyone could be so absurd as to believe that a connection between human beings could be forged through words, let alone in a foreign language.

"That was obviously a mistake!" Judith said rapidly, defensively.

"No," said Matsushita. Then he ceased. Was he too weary now to have this out in English, or to go on with a dialogue which on both sides had swelled to bursting with lies? Yet instead of "No," he could have said nothing, or "Yes," or "It might have been better to wait."

Matsushita reached for the check, leaving Judith disoriented. Inadequate as it might be, his "No" would have to suffice as a demonstration of his feelings.

On the deserted street there was not a car in sight.

As soon as he saw a taxi, Matsushita hailed it competently, in military fashion. He opened the door and stood officiously by as she arranged herself as best she could. She watched Matsushita slam shut the door of her cage.

"I will call you a week from Sunday at three-thirty," he said. "I'll be away until then with Kuronuma-san."

He reached forward and kissed her on the cheek, a kiss so soft it was like a whisper, a rush of words whose sense one couldn't distinguish, a sound whose meaning one was free to fill in for oneself.

"You're famous for not calling when you say you will," she risked. And then she sped away, clinging to Matsushita's promise like a dying person to news that a complete cure for her disease was within reach.

Chapter Two

*A*s soon as she was alone in her room the image of Matsushita floated before her eyes. She reveled in his personal beauty, even his many wrinkles evoking aged, softened leather. She played once again upon the image of Matsushita as an ancient, fragile vessel discovered by archaeologists after centuries of having remained in the ground miraculously intact. Unearthed, it was acutely sensitive to light and air, just as Matsushita was buffeted by the whims of selfish, impossible people like Kuronuma.

There must be a way back to him. She felt as if she had nothing to do, no occupation, no work worth the effort that could compete with her struggle to demonstrate her value to this man.

Now as she waited for the Sunday of his return she read in the newspaper, a banner headline, of the American ship the *Midway* which had sailed into Yokosuka harbor without having first unloaded its nuclear weapons. Arrogantly it had violated Japan's treaty with the United States stipulating that nuclear materials were never to be brought into Japanese territory. Members of the American crew had admitted to having undergone training to prepare for possible radioactive leaks, confiding that no cargo had been removed prior to the entry of the *Midway* into

Japanese waters, an admission that they carried nuclear weapons.

What would Matsushita say, what would he feel? Would he notice that these sailors had, like her, been affected by Japan, that Japan had stirred impulses in them to be frank and direct, to reveal an absence of guile in the presence of so much visceral indirection and evasiveness? Would he care? Would he see her as part of an alien force? Or would he only shrug his shoulders, as if to say, again and again, it can't be helped, it is of no concern to me?

There was also a story about a labor union leader of an Osaka transport company who had disappeared. Later his wife received a telegram ostensibly signed by her husband, ordering her in his name to sever his relations with the company. "Go there, get my salary and retirement pay," he had supposedly written. "I will work in Tokyo. Wait for me. I am tired of the work of the labor union." He was never heard of again. She longed to share with Matsushita the perils of his world, for it must be danger like this which made him so wary, which gave him the aura of being hunted, which demanded of him distance, caution, diligence.

In the same paper she also read that two members of the "Middle Core Faction" of student militants were attacked by five boys bearing iron pipes, assailants they identified as rivals of the "Revolutionary Marxist Faction." It was a time of reaction, of isolation and degeneration in the remnants of the Japanese student movement in which Matsushita had been too old, or already too jaded, to have participated, even in its earliest days when it had opposed the Korean War. Pockets of people met with disaster; no one intervened on their behalf. And for whom had these radicals spoken finally but themselves?

Disarray was everywhere; as in the thirties in Japan, even labor leaders were in jeopardy. If only Matsushita would allow himself to need her, permit her to love him as she could so totally. With her love she would shield him from the pain, the suffering running rampant in his Japan. Sunday would come and she would show him.

The days passed slowly. One night Paul invited her to a play performed in Kinokuniya Hall in Shinjuku. Her room had seemed to be shrinking each day. Soon it would grow so tiny she would be unable to crawl out. She knew she'd better go.

The subject matter of the play was repellent, grotesque, galaxies away from the subtleties of Matsushita. It was about a man enslaved by a fetish to steal women's underwear from neighborhood clotheslines. An operation, a "cure," then transformed him into a grass eater whose digestion was now accompanied by loud farts and uncontrollable urinary sieges. He was told that he would become "the first of a new generation of men." A passive person, he saw this as his sole avenue of escape from anonymity. To become "someone," self-destruction was not too high a price.

The playwright was present, surrounded afterward by an entourage of young men who admired his nihilism, the fashionable view that men would do anything to survive. But self-confident as he was, his physical presence was paltry and inadequate when compared to that of Matsushita. What was he anyway despite his awards but a short stocky man with small darting eyes concealed behind horn-rimmed glasses? His skin was rough and pockmarked, while Matsushita's had the texture of satin. She guessed that his legs must be squat and stubby, unlike the long, sinewy limbs of Matsushita which so defied the national stereotype. But if he lacked high cheekbones and an aristocratic demeanor, the playwright had become rich and famous, had achieved what Matsushita must crave more than anything: success.

While Paul made his way down front to congratulate the playwright, she remained in her seat, overcome by loneliness, the sense of having been abandoned forever. It was Matsushita's fault that she had to depend upon Paul's solicitude, that she had degenerated into being an object of his pity. Matsushita had even undermined her friendship with Paul. And he was getting away with it. There seemed nothing she could do to him.

She imagined writing a scathing review of *Song of Siberia*. Sarcastically she would call it a "Japanese Walden Pond." Its coldness, the superficiality of its homoerotic male characters, its sentimental and clichéed glorification of primitive rural life, weren't these reflections of the weaknesses of Matsushita himself?

But a harsh notice by a foreigner wouldn't distress Matsushita. He might shake his head in harassed irritation, but no more. What foreigners did or said, whether they bled openly in public or hid themselves away in secret to lick their wounds, would be of "no concern" to him. *Ore ni wa kankei nai.*

The pain of outsiders could never break through his closed circle, the "family" within which he moved. She remembered having gone to the Kabuki theater during her first trip.

A very old woman across the aisle had suddenly keeled over, losing consciousness. Beside her sat her daughter, a thin, bespectacled woman in her forties, now horrified and helpless. On her other side sat a robust young man in his thirties enjoying the Kabuki on a Sunday afternoon with his wife and small daughter.

The young man refused to allow the incident to intrude into his ordered world. It was, after all, of "no concern" to him. He continued to stare straight ahead at the stage while the woman, gaunt as she was, was left to remove her mother from the theater. Dragging her out by gripping her under the arms, she literally pulled her mother out of the auditorium, with the old lady's feet trailing up the aisle. For although the old woman was small, her daughter had to struggle with all her might to remove her alone. Was it a case of the man having been trained not to put the women in a relation of obligation to him? Was it socially incorrect to help her? The old lady might have been dying as the rest of the audience, not merely the young man and his wife, but all present, kept their eyes riveted on the stage, as if to deny that other spectacle unfolding under their very noses.

Matsushita demanded to be viewed as unique, utterly different from his countrymen. Unlike his middle-class counterpart sitting in the Sunday audience at the Kabuki in neat black suit, white shirt and tie, Matsushita, though a man of forty-five, presented himself in the image of a boy. Avoiding his son for years so as not to "upset him" as he had sadly put it in what had to be seen as his infinite capacity for rationalization, he had his hair permanent waved. Unlike other Japanese men of his age, he would not be easily defined, limited, identified. He could act as he chose. He would create himself.

Two more days passed.

And then the ugly, meagerly appointed hotel, the tiny, stifling room where one could not even pace, again became impossible.

The names of two American exiles had been given to her by an art critic she knew. She dialed the number of the English-language publishing house where the two women worked. The woman named Sylvie answered. Judith mentioned their mutual friend. Apparently satisfied, Sylvie suggested they meet at the Pub Cardinal, a plastic, Japanese rendition of mellow English equivalents.

Located at Roppongi crossroads, a spot known to all foreigners, it was easy to find. Even easier to identify were Sylvie and her friend Emily although it would, Judith immediately realized, be a problem to tell them apart. Each had straight brown hair, wide-set brown eyes and midwestern jaws; both wore blue jeans. One had a T-shirt on, the other a red plaid blouse. Slender, short women in their early thirties, their smiles were wide, unfelt. They sat in a booth and made small talk about the difficulties of being foreigners in Japan, notwithstanding that Emily had been here off and on since the Occupation, when her father was an officer in the American army. They ate Caesar salads and spaghetti with clam sauce, hardly the fare of an English pub, but this was Tokyo with its flamboyant combinations.

Anxious to talk, Judith began by commenting about Japanese women. "They're the most oppressed in the world," she asserted. "Excepting Moslems. The men expect submission and then gratitude."

She met no resistance.

"No foreign woman could stand it," said Emily.

Thus encouraged, Judith moved to her real subject, the possibilities of connection between Japanese men and foreign women.

"Don't you think Japanese men want Western women because this submissiveness is so unappealing? They could be tired of the burden of women who take no active part in the world."

"No," said Sylvie, "you're wrong. Japanese women

don't live through men at all. They're strong. They find pleasure in each other's company. You'll always find Japanese women out together at night. They're much too smart to expect anything of men."

"Japanese women have found the ideal solution," added Emily. "They treat these men like children, which is just what they deserve."

"But don't they pay a heavy price for indulging tyrants," Judith persisted. "It suits these men very well to be treated like children. So many Japanese women seem brittle, parched, unhappy. It looks to me as if they've lost their sensuality."

This brought no reply. There seemed no point in mentioning Matsushita. Emily and Sylvie seemed restless, impatient, and angry with her, and she couldn't figure out why. One would have thought that being foreign women in Japan, they had much in common. She was sorry she had come.

Finally Emily, who seemed the more self-assured of the two, asked, "Can't you tell?" And Judith suddenly knew what she meant.

"Of course."

Now Emily and Sylvie became warmer and more talkative.

"Japan suits us very well," confided Emily. "Here homosexuality is entirely acceptable, a natural form of sexual expression. What a relief it is, given our experiences in America."

Judith nodded sympathetically. But she was disappointed. Emily and Sylvie only wanted to use her to unburden themselves about their lesbianism and to approve their choice of Japan as a safe haven and sanctuary for free sexual choice.

Yet all wasn't as harmonious as they had first led her to believe. "Things haven't been so good between us lately," the timid Sylvie confessed. "Emily is attracted to young Japanese women and while we've agreed to see other people, I'm very jealous. I tend to be monogamous while Emily likes a variety of sexual partners."

Emily nodded in agreement. Judith longed to be back in her hotel, for if she were open about her emotions, these women no doubt would be scornful. Not only would they find her obsession with Matsushita absurd, but they might construe her mention of a heterosexual attachment as a criticism of their own preference. They would drench her with their anger at themselves for spilling the intimate details of their lives into so unsympathetic an ear. But there was no opportunity even to mention Matsushita. Emily and Sylvie were obviously so absorbed in their own relationship that they could talk of nothing else.

Thus inhibited, Judith fell silent. Emily and Sylvie began to resent their openness. They pressed on with the history of their relationship, but now in a taunting tone. So strenuously did they exclude the possibility of ever having had any feelings which were not homosexual that Judith realized they would be content with nothing less than an analogous confession from her.

Here, they seemed to imply, in the moral safety of Japan, she, too, could admit to her own lesbian experiences. She could join their circle. Like cats toying with a weak, disoriented prey, they tested her. Did she have the courage to admit to her own feelings for women? Nothing less would do. She tried to express sympathy for their situation. She became effusive. "It's wonderful," she gushed, that homosexual women, foreigners at that, could live so happily in Japan, free from disdain or persecution. She felt them doubting her, accusing her of condescension. She had tried to be supportive, they had seemed to be requesting affirmation. Was her wariness, her own frustration, apparent to them? In any event, it was clear that what she was offering was not sufficient.

After a while, like Siamese twins, in synchronized motion, they rose from their chairs. Then, perhaps assailed by vestigial guilt, they asked her if she wished to join them for a drink at their favorite club.

"You'd never find this place on your own," whispered Sylvie. "But every foreigner should see it."

They were letting out some rope. Judith was a foreigner they were entertaining. They must treat her distantly yet correctly; they never had to see her again. Why not then see the evening through?

The bar was called the Meow-Meow. It could be reached only after three descents down narrow, unmarked alleys and finally up a steep flight of stone steps which materialized out of nowhere. At the top of the stairs a small street began. At the second doorway they stopped.

They entered a tiny, smoke-filled room bisected by a long bar. The tables were pushed very close together. The spicy odors of French perfumes filled the stale air. At least half the women wore men's trousers, white shirts, gray vests, and black ties. A few were in mini-skirts, T-shirts. A minuscule dance floor was packed with swaying bodies, rhythmically moving.

Emily and Sylvie sat at a table by themselves. They ignored Judith, who had to sit alone. Alternately, they would dance with different women, but never with each other. A tiny woman appeared at Judith's table. Only a mound of kinky hair allowed her to rise above the height of a child. She asked Judith to dance. Judith accepted.

Surprisingly strong, the woman held her close, rubbing her breasts, free beneath a skin-tight pink T-shirt, against Judith's stomach. She didn't speak. No doubt she knew no English and considered it pointless to try Japanese. Judith squirmed trying not to make contact yet not be impolite either. She thought they must seem abysmally awkward. The dance went on and on. Finally Judith felt herself relax, become attuned to the music. Then it was over. The tiny woman looked at her expectantly, but she said nothing, made no reciprocal gesture, of thanks or of further interest. The woman drifted away. Should she, trepidations aside, have seized the occasion to embrace someone else, a woman? Should she consider casting the image of Matsushita adrift?

She sat back down at her lonely table and devoted herself to staring while the others seemed to look at her inquiringly, wondering, no doubt, if she were one of them. She felt strange, unable to deal with the sensations she had experienced when she danced with the soft tiny woman with her sharp, insistent breasts. The women around her now seemed beautiful, she coarse and unable to feel. Packed in ice, she was insulting them by finding no decorum but that of an awkward, uncomfortable voyeur. They were generous, tolerating her unwelcome presence out of good nature and the absence of shame.

She stood up to go. Emily and Sylvie waved, goodbyes which bore no promise of their ever meeting again. She fled in relief. She would find solace only with Matsushita, only with him could her spirit rest. She did wonder if it was only the lack of physical courage which prevented her from arranging to meet the tiny woman with the kinky hair who had danced with her. Then it seemed that she had done the right thing. Any relation with that woman would have had to be purely physical, a rubbing together of parts, a cold tingling of skin, rhythm without spirit.

In five minutes the taxi had conveyed her from the Meow-Meow to her hotel. Alone, she envied Emily and Sylvie. They had each other. They could rest secure in that relation. She longed for the connection she might create with Matsushita, even if it would suffer as many rough places as theirs. Alone, what did she have before her but the task once more of conjuring up Matsushita's body, as if he were a rag doll she were taking with her to bed that she might the more easily drift off to sleep?

The next morning brought only renewed restlessness. She had to get out again. She dialed another number. The evening had been so empty. Perhaps she should meet politically sympathetic Japanese, the better to place the conservatively apolitical Matsushita in more lucid perspective.

Kuroda was the editor of the radical English-language newspaper, the only one of its kind in Japan. His offices, a warren of tiny, cluttered rooms lined with books and bound magazines, were across the street from one of the biggest tourist hotels in Akasaka, an unlikely location for so militantly dissident an activity. Kuroda was at least fifty, yet he had the unlined face of a boy. Animated, impatient, he expected her at once to place herself for him politically.

The conversation turned to China. "I have strong reservations about the Cultural Revolution," said Judith. "What had the Chinese to gain by crushing the Hundred Flowers Movement?"

Then she could have bitten her tongue. Kuroda might easily be a Maoist. And it was always stupid in

Japan to blurt out opinions without first assessing how they would be received. She had been a recluse too long.

Undaunted, Kuroda launched into a discussion of the splits in the Japanese Communist Party, obliquely suggesting his preference for the pro-Chinese faction and in this most Japanese manner signaling that he would tolerate no further attacks on Mao or the Maoists.

It was imperative that she change the subject, and fast. "Do you know Sato?" she asked, more to fill the vacuum than through any calculated motive. Sato had been the leader of the anti-Vietnam War movement in Japan and one of the most persistent organizers of antiwar support groups outside the United States. At once she realized her mistake, for Kuroda now concluded that she had come to see him not through political sympathy, but only to gain access to Sato, known as much for his appeal to women as for his radical activities.

"So you want to meet Sato?" He all but leered. "Everybody does. But he doesn't give out his private telephone number so he won't be disturbed when he's writing. Which is all the time. But I can call him and invite you to one of our meetings when he'll be there."

That Wednesday night at ten, she found herself standing outside the door of a classroom of a Japanese "liberation school," watching, listening to a young man speak angrily against Japanese imperialism, the exploitation of labor on Okinawa, women on assembly lines earning five cents an hour. A woman in her thirties angrily denounced "lib" as "middle class" and "of no relevance to the Japanese woman."

Sato stood, silent and attentive, at the back of the room. His hair was rumpled; it looked as if it hadn't been combed that day. His clothes were baggy, wrinkled—a plaid flannel shirt, khaki pants. His eyes seemed direct, no shadows beyond, no machinations. He was fat for a Japanese, slow, his fingers were short, his hands pudgy, like a child's. At once she thought, Well, he's nice. Warm. Reachable. Standing there he didn't seem quite like a Japanese at all.

When the session was over, everyone crowded around him. He towered over his students, burly, likable, a catalyst for their intense questioning.

Afterward a smaller group repaired to a Korean restaurant. With silvery quickness the women maneuvered, each trying to sit next to Sato. Judith found herself doing the same. Was she more aggressive than these Japanese women? She succeeded. Sato seemed not to notice. He went on talking about the fate of the Korean minority in Japan, the single-minded ruthlessness of discrimination against Japanese of Korean origin.

He spoke slowly, half in English, for Judith's benefit. His tone was of minimal expectation. What counted first was that injustice be noted. He was not flirtatious. Man or woman, he looked each in the eye. His passion was for the ideas. The food bubbled in a hot pot at the center of the table. Was it with a special attentiveness that he served Judith? His air was brotherly, beyond sexuality.

Then they all trooped to the subway. "May I see you tomorrow night?" Sato suddenly asked Judith as he was getting off. "I'll come to your hotel after ten. I'll be writing until then." There were several stops remaining before she would get off. Every passing moment made Sato seem less interesting. Now he seemed awkward, homely, his earnestness an inferior substitute for the splendid radiance of Matsushita, whose image hovered in the air, piloting Judith home to the chains of her affection.

Sato came the following night, not alone but with three people whom he had just taken to see the play about the man who ate grass, which she had seen at Kinokuniya Hall. It was a demonstration of the fullness of his life, a measure of the many threads which bound him to others, lest she take his coming to her too lightly. She looked at them all as from the outside. Sato's need to impress her passed lightly over her consciousness. The friends soon departed. "Shall we go upstairs?" she heard herself say. She moved toward the elevators as if by ritual design. The moment had been determined as soon as she had asked Kuroda if he knew Sato.

She had to visit the liberation school to prove herself sufficiently sympathetic. In the Korean restaurant she had to hear of Mao and the Russians, of Japanese imperialism in Southeast Asia, still going strong, they said, of the disintegration of the student movement, now in its death throes.

Sato, in his nondescript cotton shirt, cheaply made, open at the neck, in his baggy khaki pants, looked around the tiny room and said nothing. She thought: I am behaving wisely and well. I am filling the ever-widening space between myself and Matsushita. And I have chosen a much more admirable person, a man who cares for more than himself, who fights for justice and who is not afraid. A man who would see no special virtue in *karui*, the cold and the dispassionate, neither in his work nor in his life.

Sato began to undress. The shirt, already crumpled, the khaki pants dropped onto a chair. She stood in suspended animation, thinking how neatly Matsushita folded his clothes. But she couldn't stand there forever, an observer of a scene in which she was not called upon to play. She undressed quickly, as if to get it over with, and joined Sato in the narrow bed. He took her into his arms and kissed her affectionately, announcing his commitment to please her.

She felt neither enthusiasm, nor distaste, nor desire. She wondered if he was aware that she was thinking of another man, even as he went on. She felt called upon to respond, but couldn't. She opened her eyes and Sato's hands on her body seemed like foreign bodies, gentle but unrelenting. She closed her eyes again so as not to see his face. She fell asleep to avoid his anger, hoping he would disappear into the night. But he didn't.

In the morning there he was, deliberately present, as if to demand that she take notice. She saw him, a whale of a man with a pale body and short legs, and pretended to sleep. He left and she was relieved that there had been no need for them to talk to each other. She had defeated him in that.

With Sato gone, she gave herself up to her daily liturgy, savoring as many of the words of Matsushita as she could recall. Every word he had ever uttered in her hearing lived in her memory. He spoke English slowly, in a hush, as if each word carried a sense of the eternal. Ten months ago, telling her that he was now on friendly terms with his son, already a boy of fourteen, he had said with pride, with wonder, "He's a man now!"

Every articulation carried the resonance of centuries of culture. Matsushita did not indulge in idle chatter. He plucked each word in this foreign tongue as if it were a rich and heavy fruit, rare and full of meaning.

Matsushita's approach to language was also practical, pragmatic. Words were needed for the construction of edifices. Every one had to count. Wasn't this then a source of hope, for Matsushita didn't use words to create an emotional effect useful only for the moment. He must have meant everything he said.

Chapter Three

*E*mily and Sylvie and Sato. She was disgusted. How could she have had anything to do with them? Emily and Sylvie pathetically spent most of their time protesting too much. They were petty, defensive. Sato, what could he have wanted with her? No doubt it was curiosity. An encounter with a foreign woman, a notch on his pistol. He couldn't have cared for her, there had been no connection between them.

She waited for Matsushita. And she thought, if Paul could save her, she would not need Matsushita so much. Caring outside the obsession of sexual desire, outside jealousy, outside pain. If she had Paul, she could give up Matsushita. Or at least not expect of him what he couldn't, wouldn't give.

And she felt sorry for Paul. Determined to spend the rest of his life in Japan, he seemed at an impasse, jumping from painting to filmmaking to poetry. He was in perpetual flight, compelled to hurry away each time he became deeply involved in a new piece of work. Another assignment would demand his attention—the introduction to an anthology, a review, an editing job. From what alarming primal experience was he fleeing? Friends could telephone him only in the mornings; each night found him off with a different companion. He drew narrow lines, he feared for

the freedom he stored up always to be able to slip away—
from a friend, from a lover, from the necessity of taking a
stand on an issue which would place him on one side or
another. How disquieting it must have been all this time
for him to observe her making a virtue of not fleeing, even
from a demon that demanded exorcism! And what could
she provide him? She must return something of equivalent
value.

She had never been to Paul's apartment, one block
from the Roppongi Station stop, but it was easy to find
the night that he invited her there for dinner. In kimono,
he offered a guided tour of the four tiny rooms. "For
Tokyo this is quite grand." In the little bathroom stood a
bathtub, Japanese style, in the shape of a barrel, an em-
blem of Paul's accommodation to Japan. In the narrow
vestibule there was a bookshelf with volumes he was dis-
carding because he had no room for them. Each friend
could choose according to his taste from books about Japanese culture to the collected works of Colette. No one
went away empty-handed. She noticed with a start that
some of the books had been inscribed.

"I saw your inamorato just before he left on his campaign," said Paul. "At his place. We talked and talked, but
he didn't feed me though supper hour came and went. I
got a cup of coffee, the chintzy bastard. Anyway, you did
not grace our conversation in any way, shape, or form. Instead we talked completely about the film. He told me that
Kuronuma chose me to make the film because he believed
that no Japanese filmmaker was skillful enough to allow
him to be remembered in an *interpretive* way. He wants
this film to be a summation of his life's work."

She thought of the old master moving among them
like a ghost, a god, a spirit toward whom one must never

lapse into indifference. Hovering ubiquitous—yet he could be restless too, and then urgent and unpredictable, the wellspring of natural catastrophes. Through Matsushita as through glass Kuronuma reached out to Paul to be rescued. His means, as timeworn as human interaction, as ancient as Matsushita's family history, was flattery. He trusted Matsushita to seduce Paul cleanly and finally.

"I have decided to do it. My attitude partakes of that of the canine in the crib. I don't want anyone else to do it. But though the ante is now upped so that it is almost acceptable, there are problems. I'm preparing a treatment and our friend will take that to the Castle of Nippon and present it. We will see. We, he and I, spoke only English. In such devious and subtle ways does my punishment work and my wrath become apparent. I trust he spent a typical and sleepless Japanese night wondering what I meant by not speaking Japanese. What I meant, were he quick enough to catch it, was that I wanted him to have a typical and sleepless night."

Matsushita squirming in his sheets. Why couldn't he see how he needed her, how poorly he pursued his own interests? Paul had meant that the story give her satisfaction. It left her instead with renewed longing.

"He is like our adolescent son," she said.

"One in whom we are very disappointed."

"For all our years of nurturing him, he has turned out to be an amoral man."

"And inaccessible to us both. But I did speak to him one other time," Paul confessed. "He called me to ask when I would have the treatment ready and I asked whether he had arranged for you to see the television version. Would you like to know what he said?"

She stared at Paul. Numb, waiting.

"He said, 'I have no room in my life for her.' I don't think he realizes that we're such good friends."

More likely, she thought, Matsushita expected that as two men, regardless of national differences and sexual preferences, they would agree that there is no point in loyalty toward women. It was only with those like themselves that men could relax, could discourse, could feel at home. Had Paul led Matsushita to believe that they shared this viewpoint? Was Paul cementing his own relationship with Matsushita by participating in this mockery of her? If she accused him of that, he would call her paranoiac; become self-righteously indignant and demand, "Haven't I done everything I could for you?" And he would think: It isn't *my* fault if Matsushita doesn't want you, if you don't appeal to him.

Then she made herself give it up. She must not allow herself to turn against Paul, her friend, to transfer to him the anger deposited like mercury under her skin by Matsushita.

"I will never understand the Japanese," Paul said, "although I've lived among them all these years. As foreigners we are regarded by them as unreal. Too curious, too strange to be taken seriously."

"I was counting on you to help me to know Matsushita," she said.

"A Japanese girl once told me she waited on a street corner four hours for her boyfriend. He never showed up. She said, 'At least I know I waited.'

"There was a girl who seduced a samisen player. They met at a party, she took him home with her. For her pains he raped her twice—to show how angry he was at being imposed upon by this woman who dared solicit his favors. He didn't have to utter a single word. The rapist said, 'Well, is that enough? Are you satisfied? Have you had enough?' He raped her the second time as she was serving breakfast. She had made the mistake of playfully touching his ear."

Paul placed his hand over hers. His gift tonight would be to teach her how not to blame herself. "Evil may be nothing more than a secretion of fear," Paul said.

"My Japanese friends once gave me a birthday party," he went on. "I had been living here for ten years. You can imagine my delight. At last, I thought, I was accepted by the Japanese. All the important people in the arts were there, painters, sculptors, film people, even Kuronuma and Matsushita."

He waited. The mention of the name brought no response.

"They all seemed eager to honor their new American friend. The sushi was splendid. Koshima and Kuronuma even found themselves in the same room. Then just when the party was in full swing, the host, Mr. Shibata, walked me to the door, and then gently downstairs where a taxi had been called. Profuse farewells and I was deposited back home.

"The next morning I called someone to find out what had happened. 'The guest of honor must first depart before any of the guests are permitted to take their leave. It was approaching the hour when the person who had arrived the earliest might wish to go home.' "

"Japan feels like a prison," she said. She would have liked to say more, but she held back her anger, which she sensed would only make him feel worse.

He brought down a novel from the small shelf of books which formed his permanent collection. It was called *Growing Up in Tokyo*. He turned to a page for which he needed no marker. He handed her the book. There she read an account of a perverse, manipulative man, a devil-like figure with no self-knowledge, compulsively given to preying upon innocent boys on whose bodies he committed filthy, vile acts. Periodically he would be beaten up by thugs, the *yakuza* of Tokyo, a Mafia which patrolled the streets. The author relished these passages, taking delight in each rivulet of blood that ran down the sides of the man's torn face in a punishment she would, if she could, have accomplished herself. Another passage described how this man spied on her, monitoring her telephone conversations, encouraging her to offer her body to strange men and then compelling her when she came home to describe what they had done together. And he derived more pleasure from such details than from any of their embraces.

"My ex-wife Alice's autobiography," he said with a smile.

Two nights later they met again.

The streets of Tokyo were iridescent with the day's rain. Neon lights, pink, green, and purple, were reflected in puddles. Men in groups, their arms around each other's shoulders, ambled along. Two young women, arm in arm, their lips darkened by fuschia lipstick, sauntered by, absorbed in each other. People entered and exited from narrow open doorways.

They entered one of these unmarked passages and she found herself in a small room lined with upholstered flowered sofas, nondescript, domestic, unthreatening, remote from any realm of the senses. Then hostesses appeared to greet them. They were tall and willowy, meticulously attired in brightly colored embroidered kimonos. Their thick, black, glossy hair was arranged in the style of the Edo period with high combs and bejeweled pins. Judith and Paul were the only guests.

She sat on one of the sofas. Paul took a nearby chair and sat back. The women flurried about her, settling on either side of her like long-legged cranes alighting. The way they moved, their gestures, made her feel nourished, accepted for what she was. The darkness obliterated the past.

Conversation began because it was expected: good manners. Everyone took it for granted that it was to exclude meaning. "I wish I could visit New York." "Do you like Japan?" Conviviality was all, and words were guideposts to bring people together. Sentences dissolved in the air. Communication was not left to depend on anything so inadequate, inaccurate, as the spoken word. The hostesses quickly wove a web of warmth, a sense of relaxation and good feeling.

Like a Buddha, an inscrutable idol, Paul sat in his chair, observing. Finally he could stand it no longer. "These are all boys," he whispered, "dressed up as women." She allowed herself to acknowledge what she had known all along. Or not known. The good feeling remained as the boy-women pretended they hadn't heard Paul's intervention or observed her heightened curiosity.

The lights went out and a performance began. The singer was mixed-blooded, no doubt the child of some American G.I. long since departed. So tall that she towered over the others, she climbed onto the little stage. Then, slowly moving her long body in undulating motions, she began to sing "La Mouche" in a superb imitation of Josephine Baker.

"Her name is Josephine," someone whispered. Impure of race and in Japan a contaminated being to be shunned, an outcast, she had chosen the identity of Josephine Baker through which to survive in this her home. Willed, make-believe, this self would be challenged by no one in the democracy of nighttown Tokyo.

In the darkness one of the hostesses had curled up on Paul's lap. He had his hand between her legs, their tongues flickered toward each other. Josephine swayed under the spotlight, her eyes set deep in her head, her cheekbones high. She drew her wide mouth open, revealing long white teeth. Defensive and yet self-contained, she asserted her inviolability, bringing to her music the poignant call of the pain of rejection. She sang "La Mouche," waving her hips, moving so that her red, white, and gold kimono opened just enough to expose black-silk-stockinged legs, so gracefully shaped with surprising softly rounded calves. Her ankles were very slim while on her feet she wore spike-heeled, ankle-strapped silver shoes. The spotlights grew orange, green, red, blue. Josephine swayed, her body defiant. She taunted and dismissed her audience, two American guests, her kinsmen. Other boys would sing too, but it was Josephine, now standing against the wall and smoking, who gave forth life.

After the singing, the boys gathered on the couch and on chairs hastily pulled up. Judith became the object of their attentions. And now they were cloyingly sweet, parodying female geisha. Their ascent to womanhood was close to perfection, their imitation of geisha sincerity accurate. One touched Judith's hair, murmuring, "How pretty." Another fingered her dress, "What an interesting style!" Secretly, each cast her eyes toward the benign, silent Paul.

She caught a residue of motion. Did one of the boys

slip Paul a piece of paper, his telephone number? Did they believe her to be so naïve as to have designs upon Paul herself and so take discretion as mandatory? Probably they took her to be a wide-eyed, stupid tourist and Paul a friend of the family serving as guide. But whatever thoughts ran through their heads, they remained utterly natural. America was the object of their curiosity, a land none of them had ever seen, least of all Josephine, who remained silent about America. Like all good hostesses they served tantalizing little plates of food, savory and pungent, conchlike little fish, mushrooms, dainty dumplings, all in tiny fan-shaped fluted plates sprayed with pink and yellow and green flowers. It was immensely important to them what she ate and then, more discreetly, how well she would manage it. Then they waited for her to pronounce the food delicious. Because they believed it was what foreign guests expected, their parodies of the doll-like geisha intensified and they began to simper and giggle. But interspersed were insecure, unguarded moments when they pleaded for acceptance, to be treated as naturally as they treated her. They were boys seeking to please men by disguising themselves as women, out of predilection and necessity. Yet, they seemed to cry out, aren't we all creatures under the same sky? Don't we each deserve to be respected and granted dignity no matter what ploys we might subject ourselves to, no matter how absurd our masks? To accept Josephine and the others, to like them, to find in them nothing outlandish or distasteful, was to accept oneself. For why couldn't one's own needs be assumed to be natural, inevitable transformations too?

The boys and Paul, too, were selling self-acceptance. It was a ripe, luscious plum, of the season, cheap at any price, a veritable bargain at the three hundred fifty dollars which was the cost of their two hours. Outside, under the bright lights of the Ginza, everything appeared unreal. She felt sorry to have left these new friends behind, but she also felt light, unburdened, all but weightless. In that den of magic one shed prudery and prejudice, self-deprecation and self-consciousness.

And she had never felt closer to Paul.

Three days later Paul invited her to dinner again at his apartment. They were at one now in what they expected of each other. He would see her often. He was responding to her gift of friendship with as much enthusiasm as she had hoped. The boys he picked up on his forays could not possibly offer the companionship he needed. *They* were equals. There was everything to bring them together.

She dressed carefully to please him. She would wear a dark, elegant dress with long lines, her adaptation (at long last) of the Japanese *shibui*, the astringent, the taste appropriate to her age and station. She must not appear plump. A pearl necklace for contrast. Stockings and high heels; she must not appear dowdy. And she had an inspiration: everything she wore would be black, an ironic metaphor. Because what she felt, and Paul would perceive this, was white, hope, the beginning of something strong and good and healthy. Carefully applied makeup, but not garish. Barely visible lines of the pencil, she wished she were more practiced at this. And she was done.

Not once must she mention Matsushita. The tie would be broken if that name entered the conversation. His invidious maneuvers must be treated as if they had never been permitted, his spirit banished and sent on its restless way.

She would suggest a trip to Hokkaido and the north, away from this city of the plain swollen with heat, pedestrian, infatuated with artifice, schooled in evasion. Before she departed, they should go off together in search of the real Japan, the Japan Matsushita betrayed when he had denied the connection between them. With her encouragement Paul would write the important books which everyone expected of him, but which his undisciplined life-style had thwarted. She would inspire him to stick with one project and see it through. Then indeed he might become the latter-day Lafcadio Hearn his best friends saw as his natural destiny.

Paul had told her to come at seven. Exactly on time she rang his doorbell. Paul in a blue kimono opened the door, his smile of welcome exactly as always. His face seemed more unlined than usual; his eyes sparkled. He kissed her on the cheek.

She passed beyond the vestibule with its waiting volumes and into one of the sitting rooms. A tall woman with long blond hair stood with her back to the door, leafing through a volume of Japanese tattoos. As they entered the room, she turned and faced them. Her eyes were clear and blue, her skin like porcelain.

"I'm Alice," she said pleasantly.

She didn't bother with a surname, as if she expected Judith to know exactly who she was. She was far more beautiful than the photograph on the dust jacket of her book had suggested. Her posture was fluidly graceful, her presence enhanced by a full-sleeved white silk blouse and an expensively cut pink linen skirt. And while she seemed completely at home in Paul's apartment, she also carried herself as if she were a visiting dignitary.

"Alice has finally returned to Japan," Paul said.

There wasn't a hint of resentment in his voice. To her he had spoken of Alice as his betrayer, a woman who had used her memoirs for the purpose of revenge. Yet here they were, reunited, harmonious, as if they were pleasantly picking up the threads of an old but still serviceable marriage.

"I can't seem to stay away from Japan," said Alice with a low little laugh. "I really feel as if I've come home. I was too young the first time. Things would be different if I came to live here for good now."

She brushed aside a strand of silken blond hair which had fallen across her forehead.

"I can't imagine I would ever feel at home here," Judith responded. Of course her fantasies had included precisely that. She and Matsushita in a little house of their own. Matsushita coming home to her at night.

For Paul's sake she would try to make friends with Alice.

"How have you managed to come to terms with Japan?" she asked. "What is your secret?" She really wanted to know. How could any foreign woman be fond of this place?

"You must take Japan as it comes. Know how to let go. I was so tense all the time before, wanting to understand everything. The Japanese were bewildered. They didn't see the point of it. They became more aloof than usual. I was always arguing, as if these endless debates could be resolved in some single, indubitable truth, what Descartes called 'clear and distinct.' The Japanese don't believe that."

Paul nodded, satisfied with the progress of the conversation. "You didn't know that you would always be a foreigner to the Japanese." He looked at Judith. "Once you learn to live with that, you can be quite happy here."

Suddenly it seemed he had led up to this to express his opinion at last of what had gone wrong at the panel discussion in Kyoto. Now she knew. He believed she had brought the hostility of the Japanese panelists down upon herself by being oversensitive, by not knowing how and where to compromise, by mistakenly believing there was a right and a wrong to any of the issues raised. The Japanese saw only the running tide of life, diversity unsusceptible to moral judgment. Any resolution available was only the willed effort to consensus, the choice of harmony in the face of the dissension that ran inevitably through human interaction.

"The friends I made sixteen years ago have been as warm and loving as if I'd only been gone a week," Alice said.

Paul accepted this, too, as only natural.

"By the way, have you seen Koshima?" he asked Alice.

"I have indeed. My god, he's portly and middle-aged now, but just as witty, just as intense and delightfully vulnerable. He immediately invited me to dinner with him and his wife and to a screening of what I gather is a new film."

Koshima!

"I'm going too," Paul told her. "Let's go together. I hear he thinks this is the big one. I must say I don't always like his films, but the word is that he's outdone himself this time."

"From talking to him," Alice remarked, "you'd never know how important he's been to Japanese cinema."

Judith felt rebuked, unquestionably in the wrong about Koshima. The Koshima Alice described certainly wasn't the man she knew. *She* must have been responsible for the bad feeling between them. Koshima liked Alice.

He obviously didn't have an aversion to all foreign women. No wonder Paul hadn't mentioned the screening of the new Koshima film. She could never show her face in Koshima's world again. And Paul, he had to live here. He clearly believed she had made a complete fool of herself in Kyoto. He couldn't have afforded to pretend to defend her.

"I'm so glad you two could meet at last," he said suddenly. He seemed genuinely to expect that they could be friends.

But she was depressed by her failure. If he wanted a female companion, how could Paul not prefer the cool, self-confident Alice, who had what it took to deal with Japan and the Japanese, who had made friends even with Koshima?

Now he wore a self-satisfied smile, as if nothing could have pleased him more than this unexpected visit by his wayward wife. His smile seemed reserved for Alice, her long white throat, perfect blue eyes, shining hair the color of burnished gold. Were they sexual partners again?

Paul had said they should be friends, but Alice hadn't responded, hadn't offered to spend time with Judith after tonight and by themselves. Well, she wouldn't risk any overtures to this woman.

"Paul," said Alice, "we really must do something to escape this Tokyo heat. Shall we go to the Inland Sea, or perhaps to Hokkaido? The Inland Sea might be best, the sea, the simple life, the old Japan."

"I think that can be arranged. Let's think about next week."

How casually everything was being taken away from her that could have been hers. She struggled against total defeat. He must not forget that Alice was a traitor.

"I've read parts of your book," Judith said.

But Alice refused to accept this as a provocation, or even, surprisingly enough, as particularly unfriendly.

"My juvenilia," she laughed. "My *roman à clef.* How Paul and his friends have teased me about it."

She looked up to the place on Paul's shelf where her book stood. "I wouldn't mind burning that thing." She laughed again. She saw no point in taking the matter seriously at this late date. Nor did she mention what she had written about Paul. Like the Japanese, she had learned not to waste energy in struggles against the irrevocable. The book had been published and that was that.

"But that book was wonderfully authentic," Paul declared warmly. "I wouldn't alter a line of it. No one has written so well of Tokyo nightlife."

So this was Paul, as she should have known. Being a friend meant talking only about the good. He was, if anything, absolutely flattered to have been made the antihero of Alice's memoir. "I'll always love that book," he said with every appearance of sincerity. He was insisting that he did and he would.

"Judith must come and help me with dinner," he said gaily.

She thought, he's patronizing me, trying to show they're not excluding me when they so clearly are.

"Alice looks well," Paul said to her in the kitchen without a trace of guile. "I hope she stays awhile. It would be good for her, cheer her up."

"She's exactly as I expected." She certainly hadn't been aware of Alice's hidden suffering. She saw herself as inferior to this other woman in every respect. Paul must have befriended *her* only out of pity. He must have known

Matsushita could never have wanted her. Maybe he was amusing himself by scrutinizing her reactions.

"You are to stir the risotto," Paul said, busying himself with the veal marsala. Arranged before him were whisks and wooden spoons, fine Italian wine, the pink veal, butter. He set down a dish of freshly grated romano for her to add to the risotto. There were no recipe books at hand. It appeared he was a natural cook. And she was even grateful that she had been given a task to perform. Gently Paul turned the veal. He smiled at her, pleased with himself, and, as if nothing was wrong, transferred his creation to a serving platter which had been warming in the oven. She carried in the risotto and for a moment it was all congenial, as if the three of them were sharing something, beginning to understand each other.

They seated themselves on cushions. Paul produced wine.

"What a marvelous meal, Paul. You certainly haven't lost your touch," Alice said.

"Cooking has always soothed my spirit."

They share a lifetime of experience, Judith thought. They're close in a way Paul and I never have been and never will be. And he has arranged this little drama to let me know.

"What do you like best about Japan?" Alice asked her. She seemed genuinely interested, and with no ulterior motive.

Judith couldn't think of anything. The passionate anonymity of Tokyo? But all big cities were like that. The Noh? But she couldn't explain to Alice how those wild epiphanies shook her. The food? She still couldn't gracefully swallow raw fish, she still gagged at the overpowering aura of the sushi shop in August. Matsushita? Yes, it was Matsushita. If she and Alice were alone, she might talk about what Matsushita meant to her.

"The cool asceticism of the temples of Kyoto," she replied, "polished wooden floors, the screens by Zen masters. . . ." She trailed off. She must sound like any tourist off a JTB bus, scenting exoticism, feeling nothing.

Alice said: "I love the joyous dance of peasant women, hand-in-hand, men banished, at *bon-odori*. At first I was too shy. When I finally accepted an invitation to join them, I knew I loved Japan."

Paul prompted her. "What else?"

"Oh, and the hot springs. They clean your bones, they smooth out the rough spots of the soul. Ah, *Ibusuki*," she murmured, a strange sounding word Judith had never heard before.

A silence descended. Paul lit a cigarette. He looked at Judith. Her reply had been found wanting. "You can be open with Alice," he said, not unkindly.

"Judith is in love with a Japanese man!" Paul announced. His tone was eager. She wondered if he sounded this way talking behind her back of her obsession with Matsushita.

"A mistake," Judith said, lightly.

"The attitude of Japanese men toward women is positively feudal." Alice sounded sympathetic. "I wonder if any Japanese man could respect a foreign woman."

Judith wondered if she were speaking from experience, but asking would only prolong this painful topic.

"The Japanese don't understand what we mean by love. They commit themselves to their families, only to that closed circle. But the Japanese male could never love a foreigner. Are you really in love with a Japanese?"

Judith cringed. The elegant Alice would never love

anyone who didn't love her back. Was she being nasty or simply curious?

"I've heard there are pleasures to unrequited love," she persisted, "but I'm not sure what they are."

"You sound like a feminist, Alice. This is a new side of you. I'm not at all sure I approve."

"Do I know the man?" Alice asked.

Now Paul acted as if, having opened the topic, he was obliged to fill in all the details.

"It's Matsushita. Do you remember him? He was a jack-of-all-trades for Nippon when you were here. Now he does the sweeping up after Kuronuma. And you know what a full-time job that is! But it's the kind of thing that suits Matsushita. He's perfect as some great man's factotum."

"My god, that funny little fellow, sort of simpering. Coy. And always endeavoring to please. But wasn't he gay?" Alice looked toward Judith as if she were genuinely puzzled. "Wasn't he at your big birthday party? What a loving tribute your friends here gave you, even if you were forced to leave before you could enjoy any of it! I've never seen such a spectacular banquet—that gigantic fish as big as a roast suckling pig. Didn't Matsushita bring another man with him? They arrived late, and left early and together. It's funny how some details stick in your memory. It seemed strange because they looked so much alike, those high cheekbones, hollowed-out, sad-looking eyes, those ridiculous Italian outfits they had on . . ."

She stopped, as if she didn't really want to offend. But she had made her point. A ludicrous choice and doubtfully heterosexual at that.

"He's more likely bi," said Paul.

"But homo-bi rather than hetero-bi."

Paul glanced quickly at Judith. With her he had never been so definite about the ambiguity of Matsushita's sexuality.

"It certainly seemed so then," mused Alice.

Judith sunk deeper into her depression. Paul had once said that Matsushita was known to have had homosexual experiences at college. But to label him primarily a homosexual seemed an attack on her. What could be more absurd than being obsessed by a man who preferred other men?

"Is he really homosexual?" Alice asked her.

"I don't think so." She had to admit to herself that she didn't know.

"In Japan these labels are meaningless," said Paul. "Anyone can be anything, different things at different times."

Had he brought the conversation around to this point to make his own ambiguous sexuality inviting for Alice again? If Matsushita might be either homosexual or heterosexual, so might he. We are all mysterious, Paul was saying, we can be anything we want. And tonight, as soon as Judith departed, he might choose to make love to Alice.

The thought of Paul in bed with Alice sent shooting pains up and down her back, as if she were being assaulted with sticks by a gang of street *yakuza* seizing on the foreigner without motive and acting out frustrations laid away for a century.

There was no doubt of the sexual tension in the air now. Yes, they would spend the night together, bundled up in Paul's *futon*. The secret joys of the flesh in which Paul had spent all these years in Japan schooling himself would be theirs, he the completely satisfying lover, even crossing genders with his finely tuned sensuality. They fit together, these two magnificent creatures; with their white skins and golden hair and blue eyes, they even looked alike.

Alice now seemed bored. She smoked a cigarette and walked among the paintings lining the walls, all creations of Paul's when he had decided that being a painter was what he really wanted, was what suited him best.

Finally Alice turned and faced her.

"What do you see in *him*?"

Exhausted, Judith wondered how to evade the question. She might win time, time for Paul to defend her choice.

"I find him mysterious. There is a nobility about him." She knew how pompous she sounded.

"Ah, you know Japan and the Japanese so little." Now Alice was definitely condescending, every word a little dagger of *noblesse oblige*. It was clear she wished Judith would just go home.

"He hasn't exactly offered very much encouragement," Paul added.

She knew that as soon as she was gone he would expose it all. The letters she wrote as she passively waited, begging Paul to buoy her spirits with accounts of what had happened when he had mentioned her name to Matsushita. The details of that humiliating scene in Matsushita's office when he had pretended that he had never told Paul he wanted to see her, the foreign acquaintance whom, yes, he did indeed remember. Who knew in what terms Matsushita had dismissed her to Paul in those conversations? Who could trust Paul to report honestly about someone else's feelings, he who was so duplicitous about his own? He had lied and pretended to like her. He had sought her sympathy over what Alice had written about him. Now his obvious preference for Alice proved that all along he must have despised her. And tonight he had yielded to a delicious impulse to let her know it.

All this Alice would be told in the *futon*. Among the secrets they shared, Judith would be the occasion of their laughter.

She said nothing and she saw it all. She passed beyond feeling, and so it didn't even hurt as much as it might have when Paul turned to her and said, "You know, I've never quite understood what you see in him either."

As if he were unaware that the force which drew her to Matsushita had nothing to do with logic.

But tonight his purpose was not to understand, but to unite with Alice against her. He was warding off the futility she carried like a contagious disease. No doubt she would see him again after tonight, but whatever happened when Matsushita returned, Paul had signaled her that he had washed his hands of the whole affair. How else was she to interpret Paul's betraying her for Alice's amusement?

She awoke the next morning not angry now but empty. The yearning for Matsushita had returned. A week remained before Matsushita would return. The gorge opened, the space widened. Her need was rooted in her flesh.

She had been a fool to expect that Paul could care for her, even as a friend. He was a man who played with feelings. Only ambivalence soothed him in his self-hatred, eased the pain of his self-doubt. She needed a man whom she could touch.

A name came to her out of the past: Kimura. He had

been a reporter for the *Nichinichi* in New York and it was he three years ago who had phoned her with the news that she had been invited to Japan. Now he worked out of Tokyo. She had seen one of his columns in the English-language edition. A pleasant, friendly man. They had met on her last trip and he had told her to call him any time. He even spoke perfect English, legacy of his ten-year sojourn in America. She wondered why she had not thought of getting in touch with him sooner.

Chapter Four

*K*imura was so friendly, so delighted to hear from her that it seemed as if only days had elapsed since their last meeting.

"I'm glad you called me. Can we meet this afternoon at four?" he suggested immediately.

A welcome at last. Unequivocal. No Alice. The ice-blue eyes of a cat. The long white throat. With Kimura there would be no surprises. He was not like a Japanese at all; Paul was more Japanese than he.

She remembered all that she found endearing about him. The targets of his sardonic, mildly agitational columns for the *Nichinichi* ranged from upstart Americans arrogant over the triumphs of a fledgling two-hundred-year-old culture to *Japanese* pretensions that their culture was less derivative than anyone else's. And how Kimura liked to draw attention to the *Korean* sources of Japanese-ness! Always he brought with him jauntiness and gaiety. His English was outrageously colloquial and he loved to experiment with irony, if not always success-fully. He was a perfect friend whose contradictions she could accept. For Kimura's biting wit and sophistication did not prevent him from living as an ordinary middle-class suburban householder. He was saddled with a wife,

whom he had spoken of in terms of duty, and two children toward whom his attitude could best be described as
ambivalent.

There was no danger of their becoming lovers. Kimura was short, pudgy, and slow-moving. Although like
Matsushita he was only in his forties, he was already
middle-aged. He was pleasant looking enough but certainly not sexually attractive. He had crooked teeth, and
when he smiled, which was frequently, they made him
look like Peter Rabbit. His hair was cut short, yet an
eighth of an inch of scruffy fringe hung over his ears. And
he wore nondescript suits which always seemed two sizes
too big for him. Sometimes he wore them over a black
nylon sweater rather than a shirt. He didn't care how he
looked.

That she didn't need him, didn't want anything from
him, that there would never be sex between them, just
friendly concern, brought her such a sense of relief that
she eagerly looked forward to their reunion. She was foolish not to have called him before.

Opening the door from the hotel out into the street
was like passing into Dante's Inferno. The rush of suffocating heat jammed down her throat. Even at four in the
afternoon walking more than half a block seemed impossible. But Kimura led her to an air-conditioned tempura
restaurant on the Ginza which was open all day. Wooden
tables. A bustle of attentive waiters.

"Cold beer is the answer," Kimura said cheerfully.

He talked about his current project, a series of articles about the American Bicentennial. She thought: I
will confide in him about Matsushita. He will sympathize.
He will immediately focus on the absurdity of it, but he
will also understand.

"Have you ever met Paul Meredith?" she began.

"I've heard of him," said Kimura. "The Tokyo prowler, isn't that what he's called?"

Kimura the journalist. Nothing escaped him.

"But our paths have never crossed. Luckily for me," he added, laughing at his own joke.

She was soothed by this summing up of Paul. She had wasted an inordinate amount of time glorifying his sensitivity. She had needed to demystify him.

"Did you come back to Japan to write another book?"

"I'm not working this trip at all," she said. "I've come back to see a Japanese man."

"A Japanese? I feel sorry for you." Then, "What's he got that I haven't got?"

She laughed.

"Well, tell me about him."

"He's the most sensitive man I've ever met," she replied. "I met him on my first trip and I've come to win him back. He's extraordinarily beautiful."

"I'd like to see that for myself," said Kimura.

She thought: It doesn't seem appropriate to Kimura that Matsushita be praised for his beauty. Did he believe that *beautiful* was a word reserved for women? But in Japanese it was the same: *utsukushii*. As in English a suggestion of the feminine.

"He can trace twenty generations of his family," she added.

"Big deal," scoffed Kimura. "His great grandfather was probably a sake brewer who bought a samurai title for money."

She would not dignify this with a denial.

"Do you think such a man could like a foreign woman?" she asked.

"I've never known anyone like that myself." Kimura

laughed. "I'm not sure such a person exists. Have you seen him this time?"

"He wrote to me through an intermediary," she said. She wouldn't admit that it was Paul, notoriously perverse, the last person in the world to trust with affairs of the heart.

"He definitely said he wanted to see me, but now it's proving difficult." She could speak more easily of the practical obstacles. "He's out of Tokyo but he'll be back next week. Something happened which I don't understand. But he's worth it, definitely worth it."

"You want him for sex," Kimura accused her with a crooked smile. "You wouldn't care if he was a sake brewer's grandson. You want him."

This seemed to settle the matter for Kimura. She wanted a lover and she had fixed her sights on Matsushita. It only remained to see whether he was willing. Middle-class himself, of nondescript origins, Kimura seemed unable to grasp the uniqueness of Matsushita. She knew Kimura would think her a fool if she admitted that they had had only one night together, and that when Matsushita came to the airport, she hadn't recognized him.

She shifted to safer ground. "By the way, he's the producer of *Song of Siberia*."

Kimura remembered. "There was an article about him in the *Nichinichi*. He was described as being 'suave.' "

That hardly seemed accurate. She let it pass. Kimura would prefer Matsushita's being "suave" to hearing about his "beauty."

"Have you seen *Song of Siberia* yet?" he asked.

And when she admitted that she hadn't, Kimura said, "Well, it seems that's the first order of business. *Song of Siberia*. We may not have the man but at least we have the film."

Off they went down narrow Ginza streets, bound for a gigantic theater, a movie palace out of the 1940s. *Song of Siberia* had been booked into what looked like a reconstruction of a Hollywood set for Shangri-la. Plush red carpets were met by walls smothered in red velvet. In the lobby were tucked a myriad of little restaurants, way stations of comfort. A red-carpeted staircase seemed transported from *Gone With the Wind*. Side by side they waited for the performance to begin, seated on an imitation French loveseat, embossed red velvet. The Loew's Baghdad, circa 1946.

For her sake, Kimura would subject himself even to *Song of Siberia*. And she was grateful to him. He would not judge the folly of this pursuit, despite his jokes about Matsushita's aristocratic lineage.

In *Song of Siberia*, Kuronuma had found his heart's desire: a pure, unselfish, noble Japanese. A Russian explorer meets an ancient Asian hunter named Momu in the Siberian wilds, miles from Vladivostok. The two become friends amid autumnal forests shaded by giant cedars, alive with savage beasts roaming free. Momu rejects money and all property. He hates thieves. "Why are men like that?" he asks the Russian. "I am enchanted by Momu," admits the Russian soldier. "He is so pure-hearted. He has learned not to take from nature more than he needs. He is at peace with the universe." From the Russian Momu can gain glimpses into the time when he will cease to be. He doesn't understand the railroad but he recognizes in it the beginning of his own decline.

The men in the film wear gray and brown. But nature is ablaze with color: gold and orange, purple, sienna, and green. The world is better than the people in it.

In a storm Momu saves the Russian's life. "Momu!" cries the Russian, temporarily losing sight of his friend. But Momu is only a few steps away, building a hut of nettles and twigs and leaves. Through the night the two huddle in each other's arms. Warmed through, the Russian sleeps the night, his head resting on Momu's shoulder. He awakens alone in the morning to the sound of a rifle shot. Momu has killed a bobcat which has wandered down to join them. Then he regrets the act. "We have offended the Spirit of the Forest," says Momu in despair. "We killed when we didn't need to." When the Russian soldier later remembers this night, he says, "I felt safe and good. Momu was with me then."

The last shots: gigantic Siberian cedars, snow heavily falling, weighing down the boughs. Tears streaming down the cheeks of the now gray-haired Russian soldier in search of the unmarked grave of Momu. "My gray-winged eagle, where have you gone?" he murmurs, and the reply comes back, "I am flying over the far mountains."

The lights slowly came up, plush red velvet once more overwhelming the senses, but tamed now by the still-resounding "Song of Siberia," seventy millimeters of stereophonic sound coming up from every recess of the cavernous ampitheater.

She turned to Kimura, whose eyes were overflowing. "An eagle!" he whispered, as still the monumental gusts of music mourning the passing of Momu issued forth. They began their ascent out of the red velvet chamber. "Look at me!" Kimura mocked himself. "I'm crying!"

And she thought: What had Matsushita, civilized, evasive, and overly refined, to do with this lyrical homage to Momu? What must he have thought of Kuronuma's enchantment with the simple-minded Momu at home in nature, a man direct, straightforward, and bewildered by ego?

Seeing Matsushita's name on the credits she had felt

exaltation, as if nothing but pleasure had ever passed between them. He had made *Song of Siberia* possible despite his lack of sympathy with Momu's appeal for simplicities. Matsushita had overseen the production, carted the props from Japan to snowy Siberia; Matsushita had pampered Kuronuma. Matsushita, competent, single-minded, dedicated, had made it all possible.

"Forgive me for breaking down," said Kimura. "I've surprised myself. I found that movie beautiful. In spite of not wanting to like anything that has to do with him."

And she thought: He is really my friend. He is even angry at Matsushita on my behalf.

She ate dinner with Kimura at one of the sleazy Chinese restaurants on the Ginza. The food arrived in chipped, stained crockery. It was authentic, but uninteresting. Kimura, not unmindful, shrugged. *Shikata ga nai.* World-weary, ironic, self-accepting, he relaxed still further.

"I hardly ever talk to my children," he confided. "I have no patience with them. I'm not interested enough in them. I am thinking of my children because I can't think of them when they're with me. My own mother and father weren't very interested in me either."

Kimura seemed so much warmer and more emotionally generous than Matsushita. Yet neither could talk to their sons.

"My wife spends all her time thinking about her father. He calls her every day to complain about the food in the nursing home where he now lives. Then she cooks a four-course meal and carries it to him. Two hours by subway. Each way. It wouldn't occur to her to refuse.

"I would rather be with you," said Kimura. Then, as if he had gone too far, "I enjoy your company." Suddenly his English was schoolbook, less sure. He pretended not to notice her silence.

"There was an attack on *The New York Times* in to-day's *Nichinichi*," he said. "Someone on the *Times* accused us of stealing from our Southeast Asian neighbors. We wouldn't let them get away with that!" And he read aloud: "What would happen if Mr. Callahan in typing his story suddenly found that he was out of paper? Wouldn't he rush to whoever was sitting nearby and grab some?"

Kimura laughed. "The Japanese are incorrigible," he said. "When they want to do what they please, they pretend to be children. It's hopeless to try to change anything here," he said. "I'm exhausting myself waiting for change."

In the tawdry Ginza restaurant she felt close enough to Matsushita so that it seemed conceivable that at any moment he might appear in the doorway, the fortuitous meeting that could turn everything around. The floating world of downtown Tokyo, a dirty Chinese restaurant—its floor littered with garbage, cabbage rinds, the scrapings of ginger root. The white shoes of Matsushita, Matsushita reluctant to enter such a place yet driven here by a force to which he would have to give way. The reality of Kimura dissolved.

He seemed not even to notice that she had drifted into reverie, that the specter of Matsushita hesitating at the door had become more real than he.

"I'll call you soon," he said when they parted at her hotel. Then suddenly he seemed ill at ease and in a great hurry. And she thought, I am sorry that I won't be seeing him again.

"Goodnight, Judith." He shook her hand and vanished into the night.

* * *

Two days later he was on the phone, restoring contact.

"You will dry up staying in your room all the time. You must see other people. Come out! You will forget how to be a woman. This is no good for you, Judith."

He waited and then he risked the rest. "He has left you all alone here. He isn't worth it!"

"Of course he's worth it." What else could she say?

"I've been working in Tokyo all day. Please let's have dinner. You can meet my friends."

He promised to arrive at seven and he came on time, wearing an open-necked white shirt and carrying a flashy red-and-blue plaid cotton sports jacket. She was relieved to see him. Even the viscous air of the August night seemed less aggressive, less likely to drive her to despair.

They made their way toward the Imperial Hotel through streets packed with bodies. Segregated Japanese couples, women arm in arm with women, chattering together, animated, ebullient. Among them moved Judith and Kimura, a Japanese and a foreigner, a man and a woman on a Saturday night, another Ginza anomaly.

On the sidewalk a young man read a girl's palm by flashlight. He held her hand, kneeling in concentration, his long thick hair falling forward into his eyes. Like Matsushita's, it was permanent waved. The line of his back, an elongated S-curve, was exactly like Matsushita's. But unlike Matsushita, whose clothes were never wrinkled, the palm reader was in a sweaty black T-shirt. She was enchanted by the sight of him and when he passed from view, she felt an acute sense of loss.

Oblivious to her distortion, Kimura talked on.

"My children call me a barbarian if I speak English to

them. And it's worse if I do it in public. They say they'll run away if I speak English to them on the street. They hate the United States and love Japan. They don't ever want to go back to America. And now they're making a conscious effort to forget their English."

"You still want to go back, don't you?"

Kimura had begged the *Nichinichi* to send him to Washington. But he had done his tour in New York and must now make way for younger men.

"I've kept my house in Connecticut," said Kimura. "If I could only find a way, I'd quit the *Nichinichi* and go to America and write books. Or I'd become an interpreter."

Kimura's unlikely dreams. He would never leave the *Nichinichi*. His tie with them was for life, his loyalty to them was like his loyalty to his family. Working for the *Nichinichi* told him who he was.

For the first time since she had been coming to Japan, the Ginza was dotted with Bowery bums, men of indiscriminate age, deep veins protruding from their foreheads. Red-faced, salivating, they huddled against buildings, clutching their rags around them. Some wandered aimlessly along the streets, mixing with the Saturday-night revelers. But they touched no one, drew the attention of no one. They drifted through the inferno of heat like displaced ghosts. Never in Japan would they accost a passerby, always they would be granted sufferance. They, too, existed, but always outside the boundaries of obligation.

Kimura told her about their dinner companions.

"Hiroko Oda will be with the man she lives with," said Kimura. "She's been divorced for ten years but has never remarried. She's not very Japanese," he added with his mischievous grin, crooked teeth flashing, "like me."

Hiroko and her companion Masuo Iriya were already seated when Judith and Kimura entered the basement restaurant. Hiroko was a thin woman in her forties with features so sharp they seemed chiseled out of marble. Her eyes were alert and intense, quickly taking everything in. Wearing a wine silk dress, she was also the most elegant woman in the room. Masuo was a squat, slightly overweight man in his early fifties, obviously in the habit of deferring to her. Both, Kimura had told her, were journalists.

Hiroko was blunt and to the point. She spoke perfect English. "Kimura tells me you're a feminist," she said.

Judith wondered: How could he have drawn that conclusion unless he judged Matsushita, absent and unaccounted for, as nothing more than an aberration?

"I've been covering a group called the Chupiren," said Hiroko. "The Women's Liberation League Against Abortion Laws and For the Pill."

"Against abortion?" asked Judith. "Are the two mutually exclusive?"

"Abortion is woman's enemy here," said Hiroko, "unlike America. Here it's been the main method of birth control. Contempt for the bodies of women who go through up to five abortions because they have no other legal means of protecting themselves. Today I covered a Chupiren demonstration. Women in pink helmets assembled outside the place of employment of a husband who had abandoned his wife, to shame him before his boss and colleagues. Their purpose was to punish him for leaving a woman with no means of earning a living. Of course I had to write that I don't agree with the leader of the Chupiren when she says that men are basically evil.

"We would be interested in your observations of Japanese women as a feminist," said Hiroko dryly.

"Hiroko has received a great deal of attention for her series on the *kisaeng* girls of Korea," said Masuo. "She was accused in the *Nichinichi* letters column of undermining the spirit of the Japanese male!" Masuo laughed, obviously proud of Hiroko. Kimura all but snorted. Judith had no idea what *kisaeng* was.

Hiroko became effusive. "My articles follow the Japanese white-collar worker from the time he boards the bus at Seoul airport to his return to Japan two days later. The only part of the series that was censored were the remarks of the Korean Minister of Education on the benefits of *kisaeng*."

"The sincerity of girls who have contributed with their cunts to their fatherland's economic development is indeed praiseworthy." Apparently, Masuo remembered even the parts of Hiroko's articles which had not been printed.

"I interviewed one of the older women hired by the Korean government to ride with the Japanese tourists from the airport to the hotel," said Hiroko. "Her job was to re-assure the men about venereal disease and to advise them not to listen to complaints from the *kisaeng* girls. These are rebellious, ungrateful girls, the men were told. What are they complaining about—the labor of spending the night in a luxury hotel?" Hiroko imitated the guide's bad Japanese accent.

"A chartered tour of two nights and three days costs two hundred dollars, sex included," contributed Kimura. "Three nights and four days—two hundred fifty dollars."

"Maybe you could meet some of the Chupiren women," said Hiroko, "and write about the Japan tourists never see."

They drank Chinese plum wine, a sweet version of sake. Three Japanese dissidents inviting a foreigner to share their disaffection. With her they felt no obligation to pretend their society was untroubled.

The conversation turned to the Prime Minister, who had been crucified in the day's press for graft, corruption, and bribery.

"The *o-chugen* he passed out to members of the Diet amounted to a billion and a half yen." Kimura chuckled with delight.

"Tradition with a vengeance," Masuo said. "And what better occasion for bribery than the dispensing of summer gifts?"

"He won his government contracts by applying plenty of grease," said Kimura, unable to resist translating Japanese idioms into English to test whether he could reproduce the irony. "When he was manager of that civil engineering company, he wined and dined government officials. He offered a minister a famous Kyoto geisha. But the man refused. 'I have no desire to sleep with a woman,' he said. And our future Prime Minister replied, 'In that case why don't you sleep with me?' "

"Typically Japanese! The typical response of a Japanese male!" exclaimed Hiroko. "For money, for power, anything goes. Why not sex too!"

Judith thought: I am naïve. She would have liked to ask about the homosexual implications of the Prime Minister's offering himself. She thought of Emily and Sylvie, but mostly of Paul, whose instincts for self-preservation had led him to find a home where no form of sexuality was thought aberrant, where people were so attuned to sexual variety that the future Prime Minister's reply would be seen as no more than an overzealous and opportunistic expression of his need to win favor.

But the others were way ahead of her, already talking about how sex reflected the culture of politics. She thought of sex as an instrumentality. Sex as a procreative obligation. But she must not venture into these waters, for what did all this intimate about Kimura's own marriage, about the wife who had not once been mentioned, as if she did not exist. She must be sitting at home watching television, Judith thought. Is Hiroko thinking of her? And what about the wives of the men who took trips to Korea for sex on company expense accounts? These women, eating dinner together on the Ginza, these were the wives of such men, of men like Kimura.

Masuo was more philosophical-minded. "The Japanese want identities, a Japanese identity untouched by Westernization. They've had to reach back to feudal forms to discover who they are. Now they're wedded to feudal institutions which they confuse with the national identity. A life-and-death struggle in which the victim is the Japanese woman. Were she not segregated and governed by feudal traditions, the Japanese man would doubt whether he existed. To give up the feudal domination of women is like losing himself."

"But there are people who fight against injustice here," said Judith. "Aren't they pointing out the contradiction of clinging to feudal forms?" She thought of Koshima.

"The Japanese never have any trouble living with contradictions," laughed Kimura. "In fact, they glory in them. Now you can see why I'm so isolated here."

"Aren't we all!" declared Hiroko.

Judith brought up Ogawa, the antipollution groups. Perhaps for some, things were not so hopeless.

"Oh, those groups are looking for a big daddy to make everything right," said Kimura, the cynical journalist.

"Benevolent protectors," said Masuo.

Hiroko agreed. "The company which ruined the health of the people of Minamata should say it's sorry and make amends. And promise to look after the people better in the future."

There was something depressing in this, as if they were all kin to Matsushita after all. They did not put much faith in changing the institutions which they exposed in the press. They would ridicule and lay to waste one government and then another. But they would not live among illusions of reform.

"We must go, but we will see each other again," said Hiroko, and she and Masuo stood up. Judith thought: They have done this for their friend. They have opened their lives that a foreigner might relax among them because Kimura requested it. The conversation had been like an amulet, a symbol of his caring, that she should not be left alone to long for Matsushita.

Under the table he put his hand on her knee and squeezed it. He smiled. It was innocent, a friendly gesture of the flesh. The two of them sitting there in the now nearly empty dining room, Kimura's touch holding the restless spirit of Matsushita at bay. She thought she ought to be getting back to the hotel, but that, really, there was no hurry.

"Judith, come with me to Hokkaido. Please let me take you to Hokkaido. It's the northernmost place in Japan. You'll like it there."

He released her, then grabbed hold again, as if to convince her. Should she relax, he would be victorious and the ghost of Matsushita would take up residence elsewhere.

"But you know I have to stay in Tokyo. I've come back to Japan only to see him."

Kimura removed his hand. "I think you are a fool,

Judith," he said, not unkindly. "You should go with me to Hokkaido."

"What about your wife? Your job?"

"Minor details."

But he let the matter drop. She must be willing and desirous. His crooked grin told her he was ready to let the matter rest. As Paul had said, "The Japanese *never* explain."

They walked back to the Ginza Dai-Ichi in silence. She allowed him to take her hand. But she found herself disconcerted; she tried to summon irritation at the liberty Kimura had taken to make her such an offer. Surely he must have understood that their relation wasn't to go beyond friendship. She loved someone else. But she mustn't allow herself to be annoyed. Kimura had too much to drink. He was given to being sloppily affectionate. He had meant no harm.

But all her hopes rested in Matsushita. Only with him could she enter the real Japan, exploring the land which was also himself. If she were to venture outside Tokyo, it would be only with Matsushita.

They arrived at the Ginza Dai-Ichi. She faced Kimura. "Well, good night," she said.

And Kimura replied with such a sense of yearning that her heart went out to him. "I wish I were he!"

He reached for her shoulders, planted a wet kiss on her defenseless lips, said good night, and ran off to catch the last train for Yokohama.

That night she dreamed she was on a beach crowded with beautiful blond women wearing multicolored bikinis; their breasts were high, firm, and tanned golden brown. Above the beach on a high pavilion stood Matsushita's office. As she waited below, a boy set her hair in aluminum curlers, the kind that snapped closed and were popular during the forties before the advent of the pink, sausage-shaped plastic rollers.

A crowd of very large men, like a school of sharks, swam by in the sea. Beefy, fierce-looking, bald, red-faced men, they were propelled by small motors attached to their bodies. They ignored the women.

Matsushita appeared on the beach, wearing blue jeans and a navy blue T-shirt. She came up behind him and put her arms around his waist. "May I speak with you a moment?"

"No." He hurried away. She looked up to the platform office where he was now engaged in an animated telephone conversation. She moved into his line of vision, but still he wouldn't notice her. Matsushita talked on and on, as unruffled as the shimmering sea. As she collected her belongings and was about to leave, he seemed at last conscious of her presence. But she had lost a package containing the books she had written. Frantically she began to search the spot where she had been sitting. When she looked up to the platform once more, Matsushita was gone.

She woke up feeling as if she had been beaten over the head with a club. Her limbs were exhausted and ached, her eyes burned. Was she physically ill too? If only he would return.

She was in bed at eleven on Wednesday night when with a shrill burp the telephone rang. Involuntarily her throat caught. Had Matsushita returned early and decided to exercise his freedom to be unpredictable? But would he compromise himself with so intimate a gesture as calling late at night?

"How are you, Judith?" Kimura sang out, heavily under the influence and telephoning from Tokyo Station while he waited for the commuter train home.

"I want to come up to your room and make love to you."

She laughed. She couldn't imagine going to bed with the amiable Kimura, nondescript, short, no longer lean. He had small hands; he must also have short legs.

The lingering spell of Matsushita could not be so easily broken.

"I will sleep on one side of the bed and you on the other," Kimura proposed cheerfully.

He had never seen this nun's bed, barely big enough for one.

"I'm at the station. I can walk up to you in five minutes."

"Don't!"

"I'm coming up," Kimura insisted and rang off before she could say another word.

Then the telephone rang again. He required her formal acquiescence, and so he began to beg and cajole.

He knows about my obsession with Matsushita, she thought. Isn't he only taking advantage of what he judges is my sexual readiness? Isn't he being coldly calculating? But it was absurd to be angry at Kimura.

"I'm standing in front of a pay phone. Every three minutes it shuts me off. Let me see you."

"You think women are not as human as you are. You're treating me as if I were an object."

"I know," Kimura replied with relief now that there was dialogue between them. Both of them knew she was lying, buying time. Kimura had always treated her as an equal. He had never flaunted superiority assumed from the arbitrary fact of his maleness. He didn't seem to need to be admired by women. He had sympathized with her in her loneliness. And now on this empty evening, dreading the long trip home, why shouldn't he attempt intimacy?

The doorbell rang, shrill, loud, over and over. She sat on her pallet-bed wrapped in a shapeless terrycloth bathrobe, huddled against the certainty that Kimura's persistence alone would make the door spring open. On some level she believed that Kimura could enter if he so wished. In the middle of the night in a hotel room on the Ginza anything could happen with impunity to a foreigner.

The ringing ceased. She sighed with relief. But now the room telephone began to ring. Kimura had gone down to the lobby to try her from less threatening ground. Twenty rings. She picked up the receiver.

"Leave the lock open. I'm such a small, inconspicuous, unharmful sort of man. Why don't you just leave the door open? Even if I feel like raping you, I know I can't. Just keep the door open. Or come down. I want to be alone with you. I was with you in the street and in restaurants. I don't think it's fair. Come down and take a look at me."

Should she admit that she knew he didn't mean that he was owed a sexual relationship, only that she was violating the natural progress of their friendship?

"You won't even come down? What are you going to do with yourself? You're unmanageable, you're no good. What will you do if I come up and keep ringing your bell?"

Would a loud scene outside her door be humiliating? His error, a result of the alcohol, was in judging her by himself. He would be the one who was embarrassed, for the foreigner in Japan was so special, so benighted, that undignified sexual conduct would surprise no one. Kimura had an important position, a family.

"I'll call the police and create a scandal," Judith said.

"I don't mind," Kimura replied swiftly. "That might not be such a bad thing."

"You're making a mistake," she said.

"This is no mistake, Judith," Kimura replied softly. "It's a shortcoming on the part of the American male and female that they are forever seeking sex."

This seemed an odd remark. He was the one seeking sex. Yet, Kimura implied, if he was out of control, he had been undone by his long residence in America. He had been corrupted by foreign influences which exerted too strong a pull on a delicate Japanese nature. Was he suggesting as well that she was confounding sex with love in her craving for Matsushita? It was the first time Kimura had spoken to her in terms of "them" and "us," "foreigners" and "we Japanese." Did he resent being aroused by her disquieting pursuit of Matsushita, such obvious sexual craving, such small regard for decorum? Was he brother to Matsushita after all?

Sensing that he had gone too far, Kimura quieted down. Sobriety overtook him in spite of himself.

"I will come up, have a cup of tea, exchange a kiss, and then depart. I also have some good news for you. I have tried to arrange for a Japanese edition of your book. I talked to a friend of mine."

Then, edging toward dangerous ground again, he added, "I thought you would appreciate it."

The note of gratitude. Just as she had attempted to demand of Matsushita that he be grateful for her devotion, so Kimura, invoking the Prime Minister whose forays into

bribery were splashed over the newspapers, was present-
ing a bill for services rendered. Matsushita, too, had al-
luded to untold advantages, introductions to people in the
publishing world who could help her.

"I will go up to your room, salute you in a graceful
manner, engage in pleasant conversation, and beat it. You
are only nine floors up from me. It seems I am affected by
an Anglo-Saxon ethic after all. Nothing will happen."

It seemed pointless to argue any longer. She liked
this man very much. How genuinely sweet and funny he
was, what an endearing person.

"Did I say something I shouldn't have?" he asked
anxiously. "Something insensitive? I laughed and made a
joke of you. It was all I could do. Should I cry with you
instead?"

And again he pleaded, "What if I were to come up
and ring your bell over and over?"

"Oh, come on up," Judith laughed. "The door has
been open all along."

Kimura came into the room wearing his playful grin.
But this lasted only as long as it took him to shed his
clothes. If she had been as stalwart in her struggle against
herself as she had been on the day of her return, she could
not have been pushed down on the bed with so meager a
tap. She liked what was happening, as Kimura began to
slip her nightgown off. The man who lay cozily beside her
was another Kimura, no longer self-mocking, no longer
the amused, ironic observer of the foibles of his countrymen.

This was another man entirely. Where the old Kimura was all quick, rapid motion, jaunty self-assertiveness,
this one was slow and all-encompassing, all-forgiving as
he took her into his arms and touched her slowly and de-

liberately, as if she were infinitely precious and fragile. His fingers moved firmly to the right place as if he had known all along where he wanted to be. He was so decisively loving that it became clear that the alcoholic meanderings outside her door were at least half pretense.

With surprise, as if he had pressed a hidden, magical source of vitality, she felt as if she had been set free. She answered to his touch. She tried to move closer and closer to him that he might touch her in those places where her body had been so absurdly deprived for so long.

Afterward she felt as innocent as a child.

If there was any irony left, it was that she had so long and nearly permanently deprived them of the discovery of all this sweetness. It had been awaiting them from the first. They lay there comfortably for all the narrowness of the bed, he with his arm still around her, she lying back in peace. There were no words, no "meanings." It was neither an end nor a beginning, but a moment sufficient unto itself. Was this recovery at last? Kimura put his hand on her breast and let his fingers quietly play upon her nipple, as if touching her soft flesh, being close to her body, were as much what he had sought as any physical release of his own. She turned and kissed him so hungrily, snaking her tongue in and out of his mouth with such a sense of playful delight, so greedily, that this time he did laugh as he moved to take her firmly into his arms again. This time he found her with his mouth and his tongue in so sustained a rapture that she could have lifted herself up into the sky. And her ecstasy was borne of how genuinely and totally, unflinchingly and consistently he licked her.

They had fallen asleep holding hands. At three, very reluctantly, Kimura rose to go. He must make his way back to Yokohama. Half-asleep she turned toward the place where he had slept beside her as if to preserve the rapidly fleeing solace.

But when she woke up, it was as if a chill had invaded the narrow room. She couldn't locate its source, or predict its direction. But she was invaded by a sense of emptiness. She thought she would spend the day walking around Tokyo, perhaps go to a museum. But she couldn't seem to get herself dressed, her movements were slow, her arms barely able to function. A rigor mortis of the spirit. A hopelessness of the heart.

At ten the telephone rang and it was Kimura. Even while she was being overtaken by paralysis which was setting her against him, she could not help but notice that he was too civilized, too sensitive not to let her know that the feeling by which he had made love to her was resilient; it existed too palpably not to remain alive beyond the night before. Their bodies might have pulled apart, but she was still alive for him. It could not be otherwise, for they were friends.

"How are you this morning, Judith?" he asked as cheerfully, as enthusiastically as ever.

And even as she was taking in the consistency of his feeling for her, at the same time she felt herself moving away, pushing him aside. His existence was now an irritant, an unwelcome reminder of something she had no space to consider.

She murmured a reply, barely audible, yet meant to warn him, the friendliest gesture she could summon, this hint that from the moment of awakening she had been backing away into the whirlpool of her need for Matsushita, his satin skin, his sinewy limbs, his lips, his touch.

But Kimura seemed determined to remain undaunted. Matsushita was absent, he must have reasoned. *He* was there, he had felt her respond to him in spite of herself, and he must have known too that she had never been touched by Matsushita so completely, that Matsushita had never offered her the pleasure Kimura had last night.

"Are you free for lunch today?" Kimura asked. Simple, direct, without guile or particular need. A straightforward admission that he liked her. It was all too intolerable.

"I'm busy," she said. "I won't be able to see you again."

But Kimura refused to accept so undeserved a rebuff. "We were happy together," he said.

And she thought: He is a stranger to me. It seemed to her uncertain whether they had actually ever met. Who was this man making these demands? He had no connection to her.

"I'm grateful for the friendship you've offered me." She had no desire ever to see him again.

Kimura hesitated, silent. She hadn't meant to hurt him; she simply felt nothing. He must not pursue her any further.

"You know I'm waiting for someone," she said, as if it were blasphemy now to mention the name. And she felt: There is disrespect in this, for he is pretending that all that I felt for Matsushita was not real, that it could be swept away by one night with him. It had been a mistake to let down her guard. Now there was this messiness, feelings in which she did not participate.

"I'll call you again," said Kimura. He sounded not angry but sorry. And he hung up. She was relieved at this further expression of his good nature which would allow him to accept a rebuff so gracefully. But it could not go on. What she wanted, and nothing else would do, was the ecstasy she found only in the presence of Matsushita. And forcing herself to remember being in bed with Kimura she felt a revulsion settling under her skin, depositing itself in every pore. She felt shame that she had lost control, submitted to feelings not her own. What could she possibly feel for Kimura, short, sloppy, with that stupid grin on his face, with those crooked teeth and attempts at irony that invariably fell short. It had been cheap and dishonest of her to have slept with him.

And then she forced herself to stand apart and see why she had done it. Wasn't it another instance of the old schizophrenia? He had made the mistake of trying to please her, that sin which could so swiftly harden her against a man that she couldn't bear the thought of ever again enduring his presence.

She was not unaware of the demons in whose grip she struggled. For a while they might release her. But then they would reemerge in full force. They would not forgive her for having relaxed in the arms of a man who liked her. They would require the taste of blood after that. She must pursue a man who could, who would give her nothing, a selfish man who would preferably offer her neither warmth, feeling, or more of his time than was required to take of her what he wanted, *his* need meager, paltry, and grudging. The kind of man who between times when they saw each other would never once allow her to enter his thoughts, who would never care how she spent the nights when she was not with him, who would forget, when next they met, whether or not she took sugar in her coffee, who preferred never to call her by her given name lest she seem even *known* to him. The demons laughed and they sent her running in pursuit of a man who could give her nothing. And they whispered to her persistently, they cried to her ears until she thought she would go deaf; she could desire only such a man. And they cried louder and louder that she was a person who could accept nothing from a man anyway, she was such a woman, one suited to a man giving nothing because she was incapable of accepting love. She was uncomfortable with caring, she found it physically unbearable, excruciatingly painful.

All this she knew, as she knew why she must send Kimura on his way. She must resume her lonely vigil and wait for Matsushita. As soon as she began to do so, as soon as she wrapped her loneliness about her, she felt calm and relaxed. Her need was assuaged. Sunday would come soon enough. And with it, she could not bring herself to doubt it, Matsushita. She would find a way of making peace with Matsushita, for once of holding those demons at bay.

Chapter Five

*A*nd finally it was Sunday and then three-thirty.
All Matsushita's behavior up to this point
warned her. She had made herself vulnerable to a ploy so
cheap that it seemed entirely likely that he would use it.
Yet hope, the comfort of longing for him, rose in her
chest, occupied her flesh.

At four the telephone rang.

"I'm in the lobby. Can you come downstairs."

It was not a question. There was an air about Matsushita's tone of command, prerogative. He sounded as if
he were establishing that he was in charge. She felt
vaguely uneasy, there had been no friendly greeting; he
hadn't even asked how she was. But he had changed in so
many ways. And wasn't it good that he had learned to as-
sert himself? Wasn't this the necessary step to freeing himself from Kuronuma, from living always as the servant to
others?

"I'll be right down."

She brushed her hair, applied color to her cheeks for
the third time that afternoon, and glanced quickly at herself in her white ruffled blouse and green plaid skirt. She
counted on her radiance, the delight in his presence, the
promise of ecstasy. If anything could make her beautiful,

it would be her love for him. She thought it amusing that unconsciously she had attired herself like a schoolgirl. But what did it matter what she wore or how she looked on the outside? She was being borne into her dream.

She descended to the lobby, heart pounding, and there he stood. Thick, glossy black curls, immaculate white pants, a flowing white silk shirt, even his leather moccasins, gold chain across the front, were startlingly white. She walked toward him. He smiled, but not with his eyes. Today they were not so liquid as focused, a trifle piercing.

"Shall we go to my place? You've never been there. It's not far."

He was taking her home with him at last. She was to be gathered into the comfort of his embrace, warmed, released, given the life that had so long been denied her.

Together they walked out into the late afternoon. In the taxi Matsushita remained silent.

"Was your trip successful? Do you think *Song of Siberia* will make money in Japan?"

Politely Matsushita directed his attention to the world of balance sheets, the new world into which he had been inadvertently thrust. She hadn't meant to remind him of his businessman's preoccupations on this of all days. But she didn't know what else to talk about. He seemed so distant, holding himself in such reserve.

Matsushita's tone was unusually hard, precise, even angry as in clipped English he rattled of his predictions. "It will do well in the first-run theaters in Tokyo, Osaka, and Nagoya. That's about all we can hope for."

"And America?"

"We'll get so small a percentage of the gross even if it is picked up that it won't be worth it."

He stared straight ahead, he looked bored, annoyed. What was he angry about? It must be the old business of sacrificing himself to the capricious Kuronuma, the endless strain of that. She wished she hadn't sounded so unwelcome a note.

They pulled up in front of a large modern apartment house, the façade all glass and shiny chrome. With lightning speed Matsushita paid the driver and held open the door.

"In the second basement of this building there's a restaurant which serves nothing but dishes made with mushrooms," Matsushita said as he pushed the button of the elevator. She was hungry. In fact she hadn't eaten all day. "Why don't we live dangerously and try it out?" she joked.

And briskly he replied, "It's Sunday. It's closed today."

Matsushita's apartment was one small room with a smaller dressing room and bathroom attached. She took off her shoes and stepped up onto the new-looking tatami. The furniture was all Western-style, a perilously narrow single bed covered with a brown striped Moroccan blanket, a black plastic couch with two matching chairs. On the walls hung framed posters from a recent Kuronuma film, his first in color, on which Matsushita had served as producer.

Matsushita motioned for her to seat herself. There was clearly something wrong. He was furious with her and she didn't know why. He hadn't once touched her.

How could she reach him? Her thoughts turned to Paul. She would share her anger toward Paul with Matsushita, the Paul who had laughed at her, to whom she could never mean half as much as the one-time wife who had written so bitterly of his bizarre sexual habits. Paul was being difficult about the Kuronuma film. Matsushita would sympathize.

"Have you known Paul Meredith long?" she began.

"I've known him almost twenty years," Matsushita said with a faint smile. She felt a complicity. And I understand more than you ever will, he seemed silently to add.

She brushed aside the doubt which warned her she would find no solace here and plunged forward. "He seems to need an endless supply of fresh young boys. It's a compulsion, isn't it? God knows what he does with them!"

She warmed to her anger at Paul for having betrayed her, not with his boys, but with Alice, so obviously more beautiful, more polished, more cultivated, wittier and a better and more valuable human being than she.

"Isn't he the sickest person you've ever met?" She knew she wasn't being fair to Paul. She didn't believe that any of his partners were less than acquiescent. Paul invited, lightly pursued. They responded, or they did not.

Matsushita gave her a long steady stare. She couldn't read his thoughts other than to register that he found what she had been saying irritating, repulsive.

"So what?" he said finally. "He's free to do as he likes. We're all free. Why should we pass judgment? Who are we to decide what someone else should do?"

Paul is free, Matsushita was telling her with a jagged, razor-sharp edge to his voice. And so am I.

Until now there had been something vacant about Matsushita today, concealing his intent. He had been waiting. But for what? Her attack on Paul now seemed to set him in motion, ready to act out what he must have been planning all afternoon. He reached for her hand, pulled her up roughly and led her to the narrow bed. So this time she wasn't going to have to push *him* down. Still, she was surprised. There had been no affection. He hadn't kissed her, he had not so much as touched her hand. The atmosphere had been almost hostile, and lovemaking seemed preposterous. They hadn't had time to restore themselves even to neutrality.

Seated on the bed beside him, she reached out to make contact. But when she placed her hand on the back of his neck, he laughed for the first time that day, a loud, empty laugh. With one rapid movement that stopped just short of tearing it, he pulled open her blouse. She had never seen him like this. But it didn't occur to her to be afraid. There she was on his bed, Matsushita vigorously desiring her at last, and she tried to make herself feel joy, but she couldn't. She seemed not even to be ready for the anticipation of desire. But what more did she want? She thought, if only he had said something to me, told me he likes me. Then she brushed these doubts aside. What mattered was what he would do. He was going to show her what he felt.

When later she allowed herself to recall what he did to her that afternoon, she could only describe it as dreadful, a stage in her humiliation, the man at the airport exacting vengeance. But now, only slightly apprehensive, she welcomed whatever he wanted to do. It was Matsushita. She was with him in his apartment and they were about to be naked together again after all this long time.

Having opened her blouse, he made a quick motion. She was given to understand that she must remove the rest of her clothes herself while he watched, fully clothed. There was a hungry glint in his eye, and she could hardly bear to look at him. What she saw was the hunger of a *sated* animal whose appetite now exclusively, gratuitously, demanded blood for the sake of blood. When he began working his will on her, all she could think was she hadn't known that such a small man could be so strong. But suddenly now she wanted to be gone. Not yet knowing that he was about to inflict such sharp pain, she began really to fear the change in him. She had to force herself to suppress the misgivings that would have led her to the door, bidding him goodbye with a telling, "This is not what I had in mind at all." But she had stayed, willing herself to gladness at his new assertive mood. She had thought, At least it's not going to be like the last time, all that happy licking, lapping, and suckling which had caused her to lose all desire for him. Then he had been like a gentle old family pet greeting her after too long an absence.

And so, undressed, she lay back, willing that he come to her, yearning that he free her from herself, remove her to a place where the responsibility was his. He watched her, saying nothing, then, quickly, he threw off his clothes, exposing once more his satin skin, the well-muscled shoulders, arms, legs, thighs she had remembered, the heavy penis she had never seen—so surprisingly big for his size. Never taking his eyes, unclouded, piercing, from her face, he pinched her nipples so hard beneath his fingernails that involuntarily, not having time to remove the smile from her face, she reached to pull his hands away, to let him know that this hurt too much. It must have been the excitement of the moment. He hadn't meant to make her feel such pain; surely he didn't realize how much he was hurting her. But he wouldn't let go.

Finally he did, but only to bend over and bite down so fiercely on her right breast that a thin stream of bright red blood began to ooze out of her. Still he watched her face. Now angry she said, "Why did you do that?" And when he didn't answer, didn't even alter the gleaming, hostile expression on his face, she turned away, waiting for this part of it to pass. And still she didn't consider leaving. She thought, the last time, no matter how he tried, I wasn't aroused. He has decided it's violence alone that pleases me. And she did feel a rush of desire somewhere beyond her, not yet accessible but a tiny feeling, a promise. And so then she turned back to him and put her hand to his hair, those thick, sleek curls that moved right back into place, undisturbed by the movement of her hand. And when he then quickly moved down on her body, as if incited by that caress, inflicting quick, sharp bites, she put aside the pain of her sore breasts and even opened herself to him, wanting the feel of him, urging that he move still closer. And she allowed him to part her legs and enter her with his mouth, still unafraid.

When he found her clitoris, he bit down fast and hard, so hard she screamed out this time and thick tears flowed from her eyes. It hurt so much she couldn't move. In his face she saw the same calculation she had witnessed in his office when he was negotiating with Paul. Now he was negotiating with her. To what end? She stared at him as if ready now for the answer as to who he was. And in his eyes she read only the challenge, Have you had enough? Have you gotten what you want of me? Do you understand me now?

When she didn't say anything, didn't yield, just lay there the tears slower now, halted on her cheeks, when she still didn't call a truce that would admit that he wasn't going to give her what she wanted, he put his head down again inside her inert body and bit down once more, a wolfish, quick bite that was a sadistic afterthought. And this time after one shrill burst of pain it only ached.

And then she rallied too. She wasn't going to allow this to put an end to her chance with him. She would see it through. She reached out to him to let him know she was willing to endure whatever was necessary to have him. She touched his cheek, his ear, playfully, as if also to admonish him. He didn't have to hurt her that much. But she would let him know that she knew what he felt and so force him to acknowledge that the connection between them could withstand anything, even this.

He brushed her hand away. His face was now beet red, she thought, with arousal. And as if activated anew by her little gesture of affection, he threw her over and lifted her halfway to her knees. Even this she would tolerate, his taking her from behind. She was sore and she was numb. She didn't want it this way, had never been treated like this, but she had withheld herself from the real world, hadn't she. This must belong to the experience of men and women, this ascent through pain. And then she thought, why was Matsushita going so far? She tried to get away from him, gain time. She must somehow let him know that he had made his point. It was enough. Why any longer should they deny that tenderness awaited them, the sweet affection that had been there that first night in Yokohama?

"Not like this," she heard her voice, hoarse, thick, barely above a whisper. He neither said anything nor let go. She tried to squirm out of his grasp, but Matsushita, as slim as he was, seemed to have been possessed by the physical strength that madmen summon at their most demonic.

He already had one hand around her waist, two

fingers of the other were digging inside her, fingernails scratching along, pain a prelude to more pain. No, he wasn't even going to use anything to make it easier, appalling as the prospect of Matsushita smearing her with grease might seem. This afternoon would be devoted exclusively to her assault, Matsushita whom she had thought so small that she couldn't feel him inside her, Matsushita forcing her to feel all the hard edges of his nature.

She didn't scream. She didn't even move. Instead she tried to pretend this was happening to someone else. As he ran his nails inside her, tracking, cutting little scratches, each sending a shrill shiver of pain through her, she submerged good sense, the wild physical struggle to save herself that alone might have made him stop. But she didn't want him even now to stop. He must do what he had to. He pulled his hand out and ground himself against her with power, with a size she hadn't thought could be his. A thick pushing back of flesh, unrelenting, tearing into muscle, leaving broken skin in its wake. One hand kept her up, the other now spitefully pinched her breasts for good measure as he rammed himself still farther up inside her. Still she tried to divorce herself from what was happening. This, she told herself, is what it's like to be the victim of an unnecessary surgical operation, flesh being torn apart as a punishment of fate, she getting what she was prepared to receive. Love, sex, desire, had become absurd. Could Matsushita be receiving any pleasure from this, she wondered? And she hated him for having branded her in blood with the anger of someone who so despised her.

All she could do was wait for his sick game to end. Then this tenacious, leechlike thing, hardly a man, would let go and release her sore body back into her custody to heal as it would. But it seemed to take forever, Matsushita pounding his body against her as if even he couldn't relate this ordeal to sexual release because he hated her so much. Finally he drove faster and faster. Only in his finish did it resemble that first time. Five rapid thrusts and with a buried, strangled sound Matsushita could only have emitted in spite of himself it was over. He rolled off. She lay on her stomach, hurting too much to move sufficiently to cover herself. Matsushita got up and went into the bathroom without a word. There were streaks of blood, her blood, on the blanket. She felt ashamed, hated, used, discarded.

Matsushita returned, wearing his white trousers. He smiled down on her as if nothing unusual had happened. He seemed satisfied with himself, calm and whole. And she thought, this anger must have been something we had to work our way through. Anger was what Matsushita felt today. And didn't she deserve it, for being so mistaken, for not realizing the man he was, and, unforgivably, for not having recognized him at the airport. Above all, that. The physical pain he had inflicted had been justified. She thought, he has done what he had to do, he has shown me the part of himself I had underestimated. He sensed that I had been treating him like an object. She was right to have submitted to the logic of his brutality. She couldn't hate him, even now. Let this day end, she thought, and we'll go on from here.

She heard a key in the lock. A flood of panic. Quickly she pulled the Moroccan blanket around her. An exquisite Japanese woman of about thirty, tall and slender, in a flowing white silk blouse, blue jeans, and high-heeled cowboy boots strode into the room. Matsushita smiled a greeting. "I see you have someone here," said the woman, unperturbed, bemused. She gave Judith a long ironic stare and with an offhand, "Well, I'll see you later," dropped a package she had been carrying onto the sofa and departed.

It must be the woman who answered the phone when Matsushita was in Siberia, she thought. Should she ask him about her, confirm that this was where his life was? To know where his emotions were committed was to know him. Yet hadn't Matsushita planned that this woman would arrive at precisely this moment, so much the better to humiliate *her?* No, she would say nothing.

It was six o'clock. She had been in his apartment less than two hours. "Shall we go?" Matsushita inquired, not unpleasantly. She found her clothes where they had been carelessly thrown on the floor, and made her way heavily to the bathroom.

There was no bathtub in which she could soak her sore body, only a shower. There weren't even any towels. The toilet, Japanese style, was a neatly porcelain-framed hole in the floor, all of it inhospitable. A mirror forced upon her the sight of a face, streaked and blotched, hair tangled and dried out like straw. She splashed cold water on herself and got dressed. How she wished there were someone to whom she could tell what had happened to her today. But this defeat she must bear in silence. Paul for the moment was lost, Kimura would sympathize and then offer himself again as the viable alternative.

She returned. Matsushita sat in one of the imitation leather chairs smoking a cigarette, lost in his thoughts. When he saw her, he got up quickly. She picked up her bag and was at the door before him. In the taxi she was glad he didn't talk. Nor must she say anything. What had to be said could wait for the next time. And she would see him again. She would make it happen. Then, purged of his anger, he could begin with her once more. She would never mention what had happened today and neither would he. Each would know; each would forgive. What happened here today would allow them to draw close, free of misunderstanding.

The taxi pulled up outside her hotel. Matsushita sprang out, held open the door, and with an inscrutable, but not, she thought, unfriendly, smile, said, "Goodbye." Then, amending, correcting himself, he added "Good night," leaped back into the taxi, and sped off.

Chapter Six

S he thought, If only Paul hadn't deserted her, left her so utterly alone, she would have the strength to despise Matsushita, exactly as she knew she should, exactly as he deserved. He was cowardly, emotionally vacant, addicted to casual sadism. She must allow herself to hate him. He had violated her in every way he knew how. When psychological torture didn't work (how incredulous he must have been when it hadn't), he had turned to battering defenseless flesh. He with his stringy penis, his stupid, angry thrusts. What had he gained? How she despised him! She felt it wouldn't be hard to circle her hands around his long, willowy neck and squeeze the life out of him. Red-faced as he had been when he worked over her, he would gasp. His liquid eyes, now doglike, would beg for indulgence, and dry as a twig he would fall backward, a dead if vaguely elegant shell.

Then as the days passed his contempt for her body seemed one more bead on the string of their acquaintance, of the same shape and texture as all the others, no more distorted or ungainly.

She hated her body, rank, stale flesh, for having been the instrument of his refusal to love her. Breasts circled by bands of black and blue, yellowish purple bruises splayed across her chest. She was repulsive; he was right. But if she despised herself, she hated him anew. He was sick, he was a fool. But what was she? And what was she alone?

Certainly there was no point in seeing him again, even in thinking of him. Yet still she wasn't finished. She reasoned that after violent sexual mutilation, his anger against her had to have abated. She would again try to reach the part of himself he had held back, but which she knew was there, the gentle, soft, accepting side, ironic, bemused, and inexpressibly sweet. Out of desperation he had torn into her flesh in a mad fury, and while one side of her knew that the book had been closed, that they could never be on friendly terms again, that in fact neither of them wanted it, there was another side which told her that she had gotten only what she deserved, that there was nothing unusual about Matsushita's sexually degrading her. There was even something predictable about it, what from childhood she expected men would do to her if only they were to express what they really felt. He had proved that he had no affection for her, but that display, however sadistically flamboyant, existed for her outside of time or cause or consequence. If Matsushita had known her at all, he would have realized that it would not determine what she would do next.

He had hurt her, but what had that to do with her love for him? Nothing could shatter that. And secretly she felt that even loveless violation was contact, better than cold, unapproachable distance. Her passion for reprisal dissipated, and she became empty of what it took to be angry at him.

She found a poem dating from the twelfth century: "*Yosonagara/Aware to dani mo/Omoekashi/Koisenu hito no/Sode no iro ka wa.*" "Please . . . Though unaffected/At least pity me!/Is my tear-soaked sleeve/The color of one who is not in love?"

Having been brutalized, she would offer him a love he could never have imagined, one that survived anything, a love the color of tears. Having punished her, he would return to heal her wounds. But how to cross that bridge of dreams.

She knew he wouldn't phone to apologize. He had humiliated her to make a point. There would be no logic in regret. And with what words, in what language, could he even name what he had done? She would never know the word for it in Japanese. It was the way a man can slice the heart out of a woman and hold it up before her eyes, beyond redress. Hatred of him rose within her once more. Once more she strove to cast it aside.

Her bruises were all that bound her to Matsushita now. That, and the chills that ran down her back, the sickness of loving him. She didn't seem to exist outside of her need for him.

Her soreness, the bruises, then forced her to face that she might never win the occasion to speak to him again. He must see her sexual humiliation as his ultimate victory. It must have been repugnant for him to have penetrated her in that way. But this he must have reasoned he had to accept as the price of his own miscalculation. A woman, a foreign upstart, had managed to gain an entirely inappropriate proximity to him. What else could he then do but treat her as if she were human garbage, a barnyard animal, a thing on which to vent his disgust?

She fought hard to remember that his value didn't depend on what he thought or did to her. And so she could even marvel at his capacity to be naked before her, to enter her while keeping his own body from being touched. How multifarious the regions of ice with which he surrounded himself. And she could not stop herself. She had to see him again, even if all that remained in store were verbal equivalents to his crude sexual onslaught.

She enumerated the vicious epithets he might devise to degrade her, to remind her of how mercilessly he had torn open her body. Words might complete what physical brutality had begun. Maybe he thought foreigners had to be first shown and then told. And shown and told over and over again until the message sunk in. Would he say, "But a woman so large, impossible!" Or, "Foreigners are so coarse." Such bodies were to mutilate, to savage; they belonged neither to man nor to woman; one could act out anything on them—rage, horror, sadism—free from guilt, retribution, or sanctions.

She winced, remembering his assault. She had never been a woman for him at all. Japanese men like Matsushita for generations had hated Westernization for marring the perfection of the traditional Japanese woman. She had read of an old art collector's saying, "Japanese women naturally possess a beauty that all the cosmetics of the West could never imitate."

He spoke for Matsushita too, Matsushita hairless, fastidious yet willful, forceful enough to have turned her flesh to pulp. The rough, raw bones of a foreigner sawed into pieces. How could he have considered affection when he would have to glide his hand along skin rendered repulsive by protruding black hairs. A real woman had satin-smooth, white skin, hairless, poreless, and without scent. Judith reeked of alien smells.

And so she took upon herself the responsibility for his merciless sodomy, the justice of it. She seized upon the very outrageousness of it as a source of hope. His anger was at least now out in the open. She chose to view his plunging her into pain as his way of defining a moment of their relationship. She would treat it as the path to a new dialogue between them. Let his violent abuse be an exorcism of past misunderstandings. Together they would face what they had been through. She wanted to begin again.

She would call him. She would ask why he had punished her, goad him into responding. She would force contact between them.

There was a banging at the door. It had to be the heavyset, sullen maid, not likely to abandon the field. Pale, pasty-faced, in a soiled nightgown, Judith opened the door no more than a crack but enough to expose to view the outraged maid gesturing angrily. It was Friday. Five days had passed since Matsushita had led her to his lair. The room was rancid, a repository of clotted blood, she with barely coagulated sores, her skin dried and cracking, her bones the brittle, dry sticks of the enfeebled. She sat on a narrow hard chair and stared into space while the woman changed the sheets, vacuumed the rug, and poured Lysol wherever she could.

Alone Judith rummaged among the chaos of her conscious mind. She must find a pretext, a legitimate reason for calling Matsushita. She must begin on a note of civility, disarm him. She would not cry out, because if she began to yell, she would scream and scream and never stop until Tokyo Bay with its red sampans and Arab oil tankers at anchorage were well beneath the titanic airliner bearing her away, to a destination charted only by a single longitudinal reading: away from here.

Again she swallowed her anger. She must approach him calmly, lucid of purpose, single-minded and preoc-

cupied by concerns unrelated to him. And then the idea
came to her. She would ask Matsushita to arrange an interview with Kuronuma! A secretary would come on the
line. She would state her purpose. Matsushita would be
forced to take her call. This was a professional request,
one that would further his interests. He had to assume she
hated him for sexually humiliating her. Her request would
prove to him how fine a character she had. She was forgiving him, she was acknowledging that if he had vented his
fury on her passive flesh, it was only because she had
driven him to it. He was not responsible. She was. He
would realize how rare a person had offered herself to
him. And this could be the new ground on which they
would meet. Fleetingly she thought, if only she could
discuss this plan with Paul. He might have suggestions for
strategy. But wasn't Paul, obsessed with Alice, as inaccessible as he had been on the day of the panel discussion in
Kyoto when, skin bleached white amid that tawny audience, he had slipped out of the room before she could seek
consolation from her fellow outsider? Then he had failed
her, so now she was alone to repair torn flesh, this torn
connection.

Would Kuronuma agree to see her? Everyone found
him difficult. She had met him once. In Japan that gener-
ally began a bond, unless misunderstanding had taken root
the first time, as it had between her and Koshima.

But she had a higher card to play. Matsushita had
tried so zealously to buy her off. He would be relieved
that she was requesting something easy of him. No, he
couldn't pay her hotel bill. But if he was so eager to balance the columns, now stained by blood, let him set up
this meeting.

The best part of the plan was that Matsushita would

have to view her differently, not as used-up flesh, but working, where she was at her best. She had met him during an interview with Kuronuma. Through a ritual of repetition, the unseemly enchantment might be broken. She would request nothing personal of him. Might he not then be free to care? And when the interview with Kuronuma was over, she would approach Matsushita and say, "We must not part as enemies." As if he had never seen her naked.

Naked. She recalled the scene. Matsushita's boredom as he worked his way into her, his revulsion, his fury at being driven to make his flesh touch hers. What kind of person was she to beg him to forgive her, as if she were responsible for *his* brutality? Once she made this call (that it was a pretext would be obvious to everyone), she would forfeit the one chance of dignity remaining, the pure, unassailable outrage of a person who had been physically assaulted. She would be denying that what he had done was intolerable, no matter that she had pursued him against his wishes.

At best he would murmur, "I am not your enemy" and slip away. Or he might not come to the phone at all. Or he would come on just long enough for a few impatient words, "I can't talk, I'm just leaving for my next appointment." He would pull the mantle of the overworked executive over his shapely head and vanish legitimately. And perhaps he would be rushing off to seek that cool, supercilious Japanese woman, tall and thin, with her own key to his apartment, whose eyes had casually brushed over her bruised flesh. The "ex"-wife whom in that Freudian slip he had called his "wife."

"Stay!" Matsushita had pronounced. He had lured her into providing him with a majestic opportunity to hu-

miliate her. And still in a way she had deserved it. Hadn't
he sunk his teeth into her flesh to pay her back for the humiliation of her failure to recognize him at the airport?

At five-thirty she dialed the number of his office.

Maybe he would pick up the phone himself. But no,
it was a secretary. "He is too busy to talk with you."

"I wish to interview Kuronuma-san."

The woman paused. She must see through the pretext. Then she told Judith to wait. Several minutes
passed. Judith gripped the receiver tightly. Her hand
filled with sweat.

But Matsushita had sent the same woman back to
complete the conversation. "The interview can be tomorrow morning. When are you leaving?"

"When and where will the interview be?"

She had no intention of revealing her moment of
departure. Then they would say they were sorry, but
Kuronuma was occupied up to that very moment. She
could interview Kuronuma on her next visit. Or they
would stall, confident that if only they waited a little while
longer, they could forget about her for good. Beaten and
degraded (she hadn't expected him to come to the phone),
she withdrew like a cornered rat biting with still sharp
teeth into the empty space from which her enemy had
moved on.

"You will be told the time and place later."

In the next hours she tried to convince herself of the
importance of interviewing Kuronuma. Surely Kuronuma's many admirers in America would be eager to know
how he had fared among the Soviets. How much freedom
had he been permitted during that coproduction? Did the
Russians insinuate themselves during the filming? And did
they manipulate the script for political ends, as the Japa-

nese left had claimed? Was Kuronuma planning a new film? Would he work again in the Soviet Union? Yes, she could fire a fusillade of questions. This she knew how to do. And for this she didn't need Paul either.

It was all for Matsushita, no matter that with every ounce of his energy he had defiled her. She wanted to begin again. She needed to touch his heart. She still believed it was possible. The Japanese were, after all, despite their seeming self-control, highly emotional. Their outer shells were eggshell brittle. Once in a film, completely without provocation, while snowflakes fluttered delicately down upon suddenly arched and tense shoulders, samurai had drawn their swords in fury. But they weren't snowflakes at all. "The Japanese become hysterical at the sight of falling cherry blossoms," a Japanese woman had explained.

All she could find in English on the radio was the station emanating from an American naval base. A vulgar pop tune: "You try to make believe you don't know me/ You pass me by and I fall apart/I hear your name and it breaks my heart." She was no better. A cheap lyric summed her up too. She couldn't help herself. And she knew that as long as she remained in Japan she would continue to put herself in his way.

She fell asleep and dreamed she stabbed Matsushita over and over while he did nothing to defend himself. He lay inert, but no blood flowed. In the dream she wondered why she didn't care whether anyone found her with the corpse. Then the body mysteriously disappeared and she was alone. He was lost to her even in her dreams. She would leave Japan empty-handed, as ever, unworthy.

She drifted through her half-sleep. The telephone rang. Beyond caring, she realized it was Matsushita.

"I'm calling to make the arrangements for your interview with Kuronuma-san."

It was as if he had never treated her as an object without gender, as if he had not been indifferent to her flowing blood, rewarded by each tensing of her muscles in pain. This was weekday Matsushita in receipt of her invoice, accepting her terms. She had been right. The interview with Kuronuma would tidy their bookkeeping. Confused by the sound of his voice, so alien (was it really he at last?) she mumbled acquiescence.

"You can see Kuronuma-san for one hour tomorrow at noon." Matsushita fell silent, exhausted even by this sentence.

"Noon is perfect," said Judith. "Where shall I see him?"

Then, unable to resist temptation, she responded to the anger filling her veins. She seized the loose end he had carelessly left dangling.

"Will you be there?"

"Him and me."

She knew that Kuronuma never came alone to interviews, not even with Japanese journalists. Always Matsushita was at his side, contributing his half-sentences, a shadowy presence behind the great man. Embarrassing questions, unlikely in this land where decorum was as tangible as the ubiquitous persimmon, would be fielded deftly by Matsushita. The replies would be perfunctory but sufficient recompense for Kuronuma's evasion. Matsushita would issue forth his coy charm. Body slightly forward, he would flash the smile guaranteed to appease, the wide-eyed appearance of sincerity designed exactly to suffice.

"If Kuronuma (she would not say Kuronuma-san, as

was proper) cannot meet me alone, I'd prefer a mutual friend to be present. Not you, you're no friend. I would only be uncomfortable. I couldn't do my work properly."

Matsushita chose to reply as if it were a question of whether he would *enjoy* accompanying Kuronuma to the interview.

"I've heard these things many times," he said wearily. "I don't need to be there."

He implied that if he believed Kuronuma might produce some new insight, a gem not already clouded by having been handed around ad nauseam to other writers before her, he would have been motivated to be present.

"All right," he summed up in his most terse English. "I'll arrange all these things. It will be tomorrow at noon for one hour. I'll call you at eleven in the morning to tell you the place. Good night."

He rang off without waiting to see whether she was participating in any of the amenities.

She awoke dreading having to interview Kuronuma, dreading having to hear the blandly indifferent voice of the man who had sunk knives of contempt into her flesh. Spasms of outrage overtook her, blind fury, again the desire to kill him, sever his limbs, scratch him until his skin ran rivulets of blood. The morning brought it all back. She took deep breaths. She opened her address book, calmer now. There was work to be done. Tenaciously she wended her way through several conversations in broken Japanese until she located an interpreter. The woman arrived in the lobby at ten-forty-five, gracefully feigning unawareness that she had been given rudely short notice. Together they went up to Judith's room to await Matsushita's call and the address for the interview. Soon she would be called upon to summon every resource of wit, guile, and memory, or else she would wrest nothing beyond the superficial from the willfully uncommunicative Kuronuma.

Even Matsushita had to know that Kuronuma's day was done. He now could make only the soft, nostalgic films of an old man no longer in touch with the ambiguities woven through the brilliant work of his youth. Glad of his decline, hypocrites like Saito, uncomfortable with those tensions, now greeted *Song of Siberia* with unqualified praise. Kuronuma was making the facile films they had falsely accused him of in his prime. The telephone rang on the dot at eleven. Matsushita's voice. Without saying a word she handed the telephone to the interpreter. Let her cope with the complexities of geography attendant upon their reaching Kuronuma. And she had nothing to say to Matsushita now.

But after five seconds, the interpreter, her expression impassive, handed the receiver back to her with no explanation.

"Kuronuma has a sore throat," Matsushita said, his anxiety marked by this uncharacteristic familiarity, for Matsushita always spoke of his superior as Kuronuma-san.

"He has canceled the interview. I'm sorry."

His voice was lifeless, perfunctory. She whose body he had whipped into submission was a stranger. Whether or not she believed him was irrelevant. She saw it was pointless to let him know she saw through this shabby excuse. The blatant lie must stand, its childishness appropriate to the emotionally immature Kuronuma, whom even Matsushita had once called "a baby."

This was to be the end. She knew it should be, she must let it end here, and yet still she was driven on.

"You know that you have made an enemy for life."

"I don't wish to make enemies," Matsushita said slowly, making each word sound absurd, voiced only to appease a deranged lunatic dangerously out of control. It was as if he couldn't imagine what grievance she could have against *him*.

"You set out to destroy me on Sunday, didn't you? What kind of person are you?"

He must respond, he must admit he hadn't meant to go so far. They should sit down together and discuss what had happened. She would expose corners of his character of which even he was unaware; that would be her gift to him.

"I don't know what you mean," Matsushita murmured.

Was she at checkmate?

"Shall we meet once more so as not to part with bad feelings?"

And he yielded, relieved, she was sure, that he had forced her to call upon language of departure.

Once more he offered the dingy dining room of the Diamond Hotel, the shabby hour of four. The interpreter departed, refusing to be paid for her inconvenience. "I have enjoyed working with you," she said.

The telephone rang again. It was Paul.

"Would you like to come to a play tonight?

The sound of his voice jolted her at once into a sense of equilibrium. A feeling of peace wafted quickly over her, a foreshadowing of the exorcism of Matsushita. The evenness of Paul's tone emphatically told her they could proceed as if the evening with Alice which had so upset her had never taken place, as if nothing irreparable had occurred. Exhausted, dreading this last interview with Matsushita, she allowed herself the luxury of warm gratitude toward Paul for including her in the circle of his unique reality. There must always be distance between them, and he had been forced by her to make that truth plain. It was a blessing that he was offering friendship, and on what other terms could he offer it but his own? Neither of them would ever mention the evening when she had met Alice. She forgave him without even thinking about it. In accepting each other, forgiveness became redundant. It was good that she had to meet Paul at six too; her time with Matsushita would be limited. Paul somehow had known. With Paul it had all been worked out.

Exactly at four she passed into the vulgar anonymity of the Western-style dining room of the Diamond Hotel. Immediately she spotted Matsushita at a tiny table against the window facing the street. In front of him was a half-eaten turkey sandwich, the remains of a glass of tomato juice. She sat down and faced him.

"I'm sorry I was not able to spend much time with you this trip. Kuronuma has been insulting important exhibitors all over Japan. I've had to smooth things over. Now we're about to leave on another campaign."

His voice was even, betraying neither embarrassment nor guilt. Again it was as if his assault on her only last Sunday had never happened. He looked straight into her eyes, neutrally, impersonally; she was an acquaintance, certainly not someone he had ever seen naked, certainly not anyone whose body he had ever even touched.

He picked up the remains of his turkey sandwich, a reasonable, normal man whose decisions were too important to be colored by emotion. If she was irrational, he was not to blame. He took her silence as victory, and his tone became friendlier now that it was established that she was not to forget the puncture marks of his teeth upon her flesh. Hating him, wishing he would die on the spot, she took his hand, skin like satin, long bony fingers with a few wiry black hairs unexpectedly sprouting. Yes, they were intimate. She could touch him, but only so long as she remembered what he would do to her again if necessary, what he really felt.

"I would like to pay your hotel bill now that you are leaving. Let it be a small present from Kuronuma-san."

He had acquiesced in her putting her hands upon him. Here was his bill, what she must pay for that privilege.

"No."

Patiently, Matsushita tried again.

"I would like to invite you to spend a weekend with my staff when it takes its summer holiday at Izu. Have you ever been there?"

What could he mean by this? The simpering secretaries in mini-skirts knew he despised her. He would make certain they would never be alone together. He would leave her stranded, his own debt paid. She would be accepting the justice of his having treated her body as refuse.

"I don't know my plans," she whispered hoarsely.

Matsushita dropped the subject of Izu.

"Would you rather go to Hokkaido? I have close friends there. It's cool. You can't really like this." He gestured toward the suffocating Tokyo heat.

"You'll enjoy it."

"I won't go without you."

She couldn't help herself. Still she sought a place in his soul which couldn't be as unfeeling as this. But hadn't he warned her, hadn't he confessed, "I am cruel?" She wanted a Matsushita cool and effective with the rest of the world, but warm and loving with her. Last Sunday was only his struggle to flee from his best self. How could she be angry with him for that?

"I am too busy."

Then Matsushita leaned toward her, a purposeful set to his chin. He began to speak in tones soft as cotton, rhythms of spun silk, free of anger, irritation, or contempt. She thought, We both know Sunday didn't count. It wasn't us. Those were two different people.

"I am sorry for any misunderstanding, I want you to know I don't love anybody. There is no place in my life for love. I work twenty-four hours a day."

And again she wanted to scream, to grab him by the throat. His work was an evasion. Why would he deny himself the joy that was possible between a man and a woman? Should she bring it out into the open at last that she had seen him at the airport? Would that break the ice? But how could she implicate herself now by admitting that she had not recognized the man for whom she had been willing to sacrifice everything?

"Can you really work so much?" she replied with a heavy heart. "Saying you're busy is a cliché for putting someone off."

"No, I really do," Matsushita declared.

As if to demonstrate his sincerity he placed his hand on her breast. She felt this couldn't be the same man who had attacked her so feverishly. She removed his hand. What was the point of his gesture? Was he telling her that he wasn't rejecting her as a person, but the demands of relation itself? And she knew. He was forgiving *her* for having goaded him into the abuses of Sunday.

A waiter rescued Matsushita. A call awaited his attention at the bank of telephones in the lobby. Dutifully she followed. It was five to six. She must reach Paul. She was sorry to be behaving so badly, keeping him waiting, especially now that they were friends again. She stood beside Matsushita, turned away from him as she talked into her telephone and he into his.

"I would never have done this if it hadn't been the final showdown," she told Paul.

"Well, I'm waiting here," he said. Would they all so repeatedly be finding it necessary to forgive each other if they weren't in Japan?

"I can meet you at ten-thirty tonight," Matsushita said when they faced each other again. "But that is all I can do for you."

Lapsing into the rare vulgarity of the direct, he added, "It will not be for the entire night. Call me at seven and I'll let you know the place."

Why couldn't he name a place right then? Was this a more casual variety of his sadism? Another test she would certainly fail? Once more she accepted his terms. At least it meant she would see him again.

It was still rush hour. Labyrinthine Tokyo, the cars, the streets, the city conspiring every minute to keep people apart. Paul, having waited at her hotel for an hour, sat on a couch, his legs crossed. Irritation flickered about the corners of his mouth. His blue eyes were opaque.

"Well, did you achieve anything?" he began. "It's easy to be affectionate in coffee shops."

She hadn't told him what had happened the past Sunday, just as she had never admitted how hurt she had been when he and Alice had seemed to turn against her. Affectionate indeed!

"I'm seeing him again later," she brought forth triumphantly, as if this victory warranted her lateness. "It will be for the last time," she added, to appease him, hoping still that it wasn't true.

"There isn't much time left for dinner." That was all he said. He would wait out her illness, the kindly friend ubiquitous in the sickroom, confident that sooner or later the fever would break.

At the garish Wienerwald, over greasy fried cutlets and cold mashed potatoes, Paul offered a last challenge, a final test of her mettle. "I can think of one redeeming gesture. We can get through the evening without your calling him. Leave Japan without another sound."

And she realized. This was precisely what Matsushita had intended. By not specifying where they should meet he had been providing her with an opportunity to be restored to dignity. He was making amends. By asking her to call him again, he had offered her a choice.

It was no good.

"I must see him one more time. It makes me happy. I can't help it," she said.

"Then you must."

He continued eating as if to underline the insignificance of whatever she did now. If Paul had known how Matsushita had behaved last Sunday, would he have tried to prevent her from calling? It occurred to her that on some level Paul would enjoy those gory details. He might even conclude from an account of that sex Matsushita's essential homosexuality. No, Paul must never know.

They walked to the theater. She spotted a ten-yen coin box. She didn't even try to resist. She dialed the number of Matsushita's office.

A brusque voice replied in Japanese, a voice exactly like Matsushita's.

"Where shall we meet?" she blurted out in English,

self-conscious, hating herself more for this ignominy than when she had submitted her body to his will. "You told me to call to arrange where we should meet."

The man on the other end was not Matsushita. Yet he didn't even appear to be surprised by her hysteria. He must know how she had pursued his colleague. She burned with shame.

Matsushita came on the line. Matter-of-factly, with no greeting, he suggested a place as tawdry as the stale dining room of the Diamond Hotel. She was to stand and wait for him on a street corner in Shinjuku, the student quarter which stayed open late.

Paul remained expressionless. They walked the few remaining steps to the little theater.

The play was about a soul trapped in hell. Presented with the unforeseen opportunity to return to earth, with the gift of another life to live, the soul turned it down, so intolerable was the thought of enduring the pain of still another human travail. The decision was enacted by one lone male dancer. He writhed and twisted his limbs with ambivalent intensity. And then he chose to make his peace with hell, the prison with which he had become familiar. The reassuring sanctuary of hell was preferable to the vicissitudes of this life on earth.

The dancer was tall for a Japanese, lithe yet strong and sinewy. His thick black hair, full sensual lips, and high cheekbones made him seem so like Matsushita that it was as if her demon lover were dancing naked before her eyes, taunting her with his inaccessible sexuality, his body that would maim her if she came too near. The dancer's body became covered in sweat as he recapitulated all the suffering of this world which had driven him to choose hell as his home. He danced to remind himself of the pain of this life on earth so as to fortify himself against the temptation of accepting another human sentence. His suffering was hers, hers the anguish of longing for a man exactly like him (though not exactly, for at one point Paul, scenting danger, had whispered that his friend, the dancer, was gay). It was Matsushita's suffering too. They had all been caught beyond choice, in the fate of their having encountered each other, in the pain of their first solitary visit to this earth.

The dance over, she bid Paul a hasty good night and rushed for a taxi.

Bitterly she had to conclude it was fitting that in this final hour of her humiliation she should arrive before Matsushita and so be obliged to stand waiting, alone and vulnerable on a deserted street corner. A man heavily drunk, bloated and red-faced, hissed for her to come along with him. She walked around the block twice. Matsushita mustn't come upon her waiting. The man trailed crookedly along behind her. Finally he gave up, vanishing into the night.

Matsushita arrived on foot. She had hoped he would bring his car. Sitting together in a private space might restore them to tenderness if only because they had exhausted violence and will. But he had deliberately left his car behind. He remained as repelled as he had been last week. Or did he fear she would retaliate with a sexual outrage of her own now that she had time to gather the clouds of her anger? He was to have the final word. They would never touch again.

Matsushita's eyes darted right and left as he searched for an open coffee shop. It was nearly eleven. Tokyo's restaurants were long since shut up for the night. At last he spotted one and marched boldly in ahead of her. The waiters stood around sullenly, impatient to go home. They glanced at Judith and Matsushita with suspicion, this incongruous pair, a foreigner and a Japanese.

At the tiny table she was eye to eye with Matsushita. But she was so bereft she could scarcely speak. With Matsushita only inches away her mind was a blank. What was she doing here? What was there to say? And who was this boy-man facing her?

"What will you have?"

She shook her head.

Irritated, Matsushita ordered a cheese sandwich for himself, coffee and Sambuca for them both. When the order arrived, he pushed the sandwich to the center of the table. Sand-colored bread, orange cheese, the whole vapid, paper-thin, dry as sawdust. To touch it seemed at once to accept everything on Matsushita's terms. She shook her head again. Matsushita gestured impatiently.

"You never eat when you're with me."

He sipped the Sambuca. She would leave hers untouched. No farewell toast to this twisted and deformed connection, this man sitting there so calmly, he who had taunted her with the degree to which he found her desire for him an irresistible provocation for aggression.

But Matsushita proposed no toast. Nor would he even acknowledge that the drinks meant anything special.

Left to do whatever talking there would be, he suddenly began to ply her with superficial questions, as if they had just met. But always his questions bore on her imminent departure.

"What is your apartment in America like?" he began, as if willing her back where she belonged.

"It's nothing special. You wouldn't like it," she said.

In replying at all, she was abasing herself, for she

knew he had never given a thought to where she lived. Was he reminding her of the scene in *his* apartment? Was he hinting at what he would do again if she didn't get out of here?

"When are you leaving?"

"Tomorrow."

"By which flight?"

He kept it up. She tossed back half-sentence replies. Even these were exhausting. And yet it was as if he weren't even there with her. She was alone at last, the ordeal over. No energy remained to her to request, now, finally, the explanation for his change of heart. He was not involved enough with her for an explanation even to exist.

"You're going to be famous soon," Matsushita asserted.

I'm not entirely cold, not completely without feeling, he seemed to say. I really hope you'll find the solace of renown. Wouldn't that be more than adequate compensation for the love I could never offer you?

He seemed pathetic. She disliked herself for making him a pathetic participant in this ordeal. Bravely Matsushita kept up his smile, now frozen, like congealed icing on a cake. There was no point in telling him that she didn't want to be famous, that she never would be anyway, or that whatever he really believed (and who could know?) notoriety was a sorry substitute for love. She withdrew, coldly appraising him, submitting to flashes of anger at this contemptible creature sitting there judging her by himself, believing fame could ever compensate for the inability to care for another human being.

It was long past the hour of closing. They were all but ushered out into the street by a pair of unceremonious waiters. Matsushita stepped off the curb and hailed a taxi.

So this is the end, she thought, echoing what characters in Ozu films said when a loved one died. She would be planted in one more taxi and dispatched like a misaddressed package to the Ginza Dai-Ichi. Words, illumination, explanations—they were only for those whose understanding was already so exquisite that language was superfluous. She hated herself for having always to put everything into words. Illusory preservers of sanity, sentences were only empty constructs which could mean nothing to Matsushita, who found absurd dependence upon anything so unreliable, so vulgar and unworthy, so utterly alien to his nature as language. Without harmony, words had doubly to be mistrusted. But would any explanation erase what he had done? If he said, I hurt you, I made your blood run only to free you from me, to break this dread enchantment, would she have felt better?

Matsushita remained silent. But as she stepped into the taxi, there he was getting in with her. Side by side they sat in the back seat. He placed his arm firmly around her shoulders. Was it pity, an emotion of which he seemed incapable? She was relieved that he was not gone from her yet.

They drove along streets black and unfamiliar. What destination could Matsushita be planning? Under the guise of this seeming intimacy, she ventured a question.

"Why didn't Kuronuma see me? Surely he couldn't have had a sore throat or so bad a cold that he was incapable of being interviewed. These are a child's excuses."

Matsushita dropped the pretense of Kuronuma's illness.

"He doesn't understand you," he said, his face almost collapsing into old age before her eyes. His despair appeared to reflect an accumulation of centuries of frustration. "He read your book but he didn't understand it."

Should she ask what Kuronuma hadn't understood?

She thought she had praised him, made much of his career. Had he misunderstood the press reports of the panel discussion in Kyoto? She had defended him passionately. Saito had been contemptuous. Had Saito over a night of whiskey and reminiscing with Kuronuma misrepresented what had occurred?

But it was as pointless to ask Matsushita why Kuronuma mistrusted her as it would be for her to convince Kuronuma of her good will once he had made up his mind that she was an enemy. It was as futile as using words—language—to find out how Matsushita had come to despise her flesh and bone.

It was all fated. She would never know what poison the snake Saito had poured into Kuronuma's ear. Matsushita had broken the rules, been disloyal, admitted to a stranger and a foreigner that Kuronuma, his superior, had lied about why he canceled an interview. Matsushita, she saw, had been unorthodox, however, for the sake of another end. For he was also confessing that he, too, had hidden behind barely credible excuses. As she must accept Kuronuma's reason for canceling the interview, so she must end it with Matsushita without an explanation. She and he would never overcome the barriers that separated them.

The same Matsushita who viciously had treated her to sex fueled by hatred was also too cordial to allow her to depart entirely empty-handed. And so this admission, that Kuronuma was not really sick but had perceived her incorrectly, having been misled, was to make up if not for the pain, then for the inconvenience she had been caused.

They reached Shibuya, Matsushita's neighborhood. It was wildly improbable that he could be planning a repeat performance of last Sunday. Yet why had he brought her here, so far from her hotel and to a place so dark and deserted that there could be no coffee shop in which they could once more face each other in silence? She felt a slight flutter of hope. Was he planning to exchange violence for tenderness, offer her a night of love sweet and gentle if only so that she would go away certain that she would never understand him?

They got out of the taxi. Matsushita indicated that they were to walk around the park. There wasn't another human being in sight, no sign of human habitation.

"Are you working on a new book?"

Matsushita again began to make conversation in the tones of a newly introduced acquaintance at a cocktail party.

"I'm writing a book about my impressions of Japan," she lied. "An alien woman exploring a distant planet ruled by men."

It seemed important now that Matsushita believe she was self-sufficient. She did have a life apart from him. She would risk his relief that she had other things on her mind besides him.

"When will it be finished?"

She laughed at his predictability and lied again. "In six months."

If she had said six weeks or six days, it would all be the same. What did he care?

They kept on walking. Matsushita kept his arm around her. Then, without knowing she was about to do it, she turned and faced Matsushita, holding her purse up to her chest as if she were warding off a fatal blow.

"I'll never see you again!" she wailed.

For such unthreatening confusion, for such profound passivity, accepting even his sexual bullying as nothing less than natural, Matsushita was grateful. And he was prepared. He kissed her gently on the forehead and then, with just the slightest firmness, on the mouth. A victorious Matsushita thanked his adversary for introducing the subject of their parting, so preferable to his having had to do it himself. His fear that she might make a last-minute plea that he see her again, that she might attempt to resurrect everything, had been allayed. As she had not fought against what he did to her in his bed, so she had accepted her destiny. He need provide no explanation, not for his change of heart, not for his indifference, not for his violence.

Matsushita's whole body seemed to relax. He might have been injected in the thigh with a drug, his tension dissipated so quickly. At the point of being extricated at last, he became—himself. With the end in sight, he was once again the coquette, seductive, tempting, and utterly without sincerity.

"You will, you will," he breathed, half-laughing, reassuring, promising.

She knew she must leave it at this, end as they had begun. But now, as if she had completely forgotten that he had bruised her body, humiliated her, she brushed aside all that and wanted him just as much as she had on that day when greedy with expectation she had disembarked at Haneda Airport and out of some inexplicable paralysis, had failed to recognize—Matsushita himself. If he would make her another promise, even one stretching over seas and continents and into the future, she would believe it. If he would make his lie palpable, she would cling to it like a drowning swimmer and paddle away from Japan kept aloft by that barely sufficient buoy, as if it were a precious antique wrapped in the Japanese manner in that piece of cloth called a *furoshiki* knotted to express the tie of friend-ship.

"When? When?" she pleaded.

"Wait! Wait!" Matsushita decreed with an amused smile, tolerant of her perpetual impatience. And she saw him summon this transient semblance of frankness to cam-ouflage his determination to see himself through the terri-ble final moments of his ordeal. Under the guise of acceptance he would reject her again. Nothing would seem final or irrevocable or so definite that he could be called to account for it.

Did he really believe it was less cruel to say "wait" than to tell her he would never see her again? Or did he choose words pregnant with possibility while packing her off once and for all because this was more cruel, more exquisitely punishing to someone who had so unpleasantly inconvenienced him? Was this another version of the rape, the sexual rampage through which he told her that he could never see her as a woman? She would never know.

"As for knowing what it all means," Paul had written ages ago, *"and where it all stands, well, you are barking up the wrong country. You will NEVER know. So be content with that."*

Matsushita scouted for a taxi. Deserted streets, yet dozens of taxis were cruising by. The drivers, fellow Japa-nese males complicit in bearing away this unwelcome guest.

She hesitated a moment before getting into the taxi.

"I will not accompany you to your hotel," Matsushita said briskly and a bit too loudly. "Ginza Dai-Ichi!"

It was indeed and at last the end. She returned to her garish hotel, commodious lobby concealing a rats' maze of cubbyholes above. Drifting off to sleep, for sleep would come easily now, she called back from memory Paul's words:

"He's unworthy, not bad, unworthy."

And she heard Matsushita whispering what must have been the truth. *"Didn't Paul tell you? I don't love anyone."*

And when willfully she had refused to believe him, he had spoken words by which she would have to remember him.

"It will not be for the entire night."

Part
Five

Chapter One

*A*t eight the next morning Paul telephoned.

"I still love him," she moaned, more out of habit than conviction. Then she tried to make the only speech which would make her seem less than a total fool. "Don't be angry with him when I'm gone. It was all my fault."

"Obsession and masochism go hand in hand, don't they?" Paul said lightly. "But I can see it's still no good telling you that. I have a better idea. I'm inviting you to the jungle baths at Ibusuki."

"Ibusuki?" she echoed. She tried to visualize the word but kept mixing up the vowels.

"I'll call and get the tickets. All you have to do is change your reservation and check out. I can't allow you to leave Japan without coming with me."

He waited, testing whether she were finally among the living. All along he had been patiently waiting to see her through. He could step back into her path only once she had truly set herself in the direction of home. "We can be there by tonight. We'll check your suitcases at the airport. Any clothes you need will be provided at the hotel."

Then the mischief that was his best friend and defense reasserting itself, he added, "Ibusuki is one of the

231

few places left in Japan where there is still mixed bath-
ing."

The journey with Paul to Ibusuki took an entire day.
First a bus to the airport, then a plane to Kagoshima, then
a taxi to the dock where they were swept across the surface of Kagoshima Bay in a hydrofoil boat. Everything
seemed natural and inevitable, even this walking on the
waters, taken for granted but no less a miracle of release.
The cries of birds filled the air, wild and free. She could
not remember ever before in Japan hearing the call of
birds. Concealed in the lush foliage of Kyushu, they called
an important message to each other. Once they had
warned of the arrival in their land of foreign invaders, Por-
tuguese Catholics. Today it was only Judith and Paul, benign foreigners come to pay homage, passing beyond the
overcrowding and the desperation of the cities to another
Japan. Here a museum of erotic art, another rare survival,
stood in homage of its own, defying the view that fidelity
to the senses was vestigial. In a building designed like a
temple, the sensuous writhings of men and women overcome by sexuality amiably coexisted with a souvenir stand
offering keychains in the shape of miniature penises. This
was Japan—where the anomaly of the vulgar side by side
with the sublime was accepted as inevitable, as natural.

Their hotel was the Ibusuki Kanko, with its tower-
like protuberance and two undulating wings, a grander
version of the Ginza Dai-Ichi, Miami Beach defying rural
Kagoshima. The plastic lobby offered fake leather chairs
occupied by blank-faced businessmen. And beyond the
lobby was a supermarket-sized gift shop where salt-water
taffy mixed with the rough carved dolls of native Kagoshima.

The rooms looked out over a gleaming, uninhabited

sea, framed by bright red bougainvillea and pink hibiscus, the flowers of Africa and the beginning of time. On their beds lay kimonos, identical for men and women. Only the color of the belt and the more elaborate manner in which it was to be tied on a woman distinguished the sexes, for unfettered sensuality was synonymous here with androgyny. The entire range of erotic response was available to all, without enslavement to accidents of gender.

Here Paul, the foreigner who had been in Japan long enough to appreciate every rock and crevice of his foreignness, was more at home than anywhere in the world. At the level of the baths, located in the pit of the hotel, they had to separate, for the lockers were segregated. The new Japan had not ceased its encroachment on the old. But no matter.

Emerging from the locker room at the head of a flight of spiral stairs, she beheld the baths, in a greenhouse, carved into rock, filled with palms and lush green foliage—a vision of Henri Rousseau's come to life. Some were as big as swimming pools, the open public waters of Rome. Others were tiny pools big enough only for two, who could cavort concealed amidst the dense greenery. They were round, they were oval, they were square, egg-shaped, pear-shaped, microcosms of the varieties of the human body. Mysterious vapors wafted like clouds over the hottest of the baths as each oozed its own particular healing formula. And each emitted a different scent, the rot of sulfur, the purifying astringent fumes of salt, mineral smells without name or identification, each with its unique power to penetrate the bones, and the soul.

It was ironic that she should have come here with Paul, with whom her relation was so chaste. Yet that was fitting too, for Ibusuki offered chaste sensuality, the *karui*

Matsushita had invoked. If he had meant by *karui* a higher notion of affection, one untainted by excesses of over-heated need, excess baggage from an unpurged past, perhaps he had been right and she too freighted with an unresolved history to know it.

She stood at the top of the staircase peering down. Beside her, just outside the women's locker room, were a few small, round, tepid baths. These were reserved for women too shy, too alienated, or too uninterested to bathe below with the men. And it seemed that most of the women felt this way, for these uninviting pools were crowded to capacity with shiny bodies, women laughing and gossiping, well-adjusted denizens of a world after the fall who had found respite in a garden of Eden barren of men at the southernmost tip of Japan.

And wasn't she one of them? Hadn't she, too, become alienated from heterosexual combat, hadn't she been shamed by Matsushita into facing that nothing she could do would touch his heart? Splashing about together, washing each other, young, old, middle-aged, these Japanese women had found trust among those of their kind; they had worked their way to freedom from the need for sustained intimacy from men who were unable to give it. Their Japan was postsamurai, posturban; they knew they could never return to the sexual innocence of the primitive island paradise of which Ibusuki could be only a reminder.

She hesitated among the women. She could remain among them, they would joke about her foreign proportions, kindly, they would accept her. But not one of them would accompany her down the long stairway to the baths where naked men moved briskly from one pool to another. This was their way of tolerating the recalcitrance of the Matsushitas whom they could only temporarily avoid. But they would never ask of such men what they could not or would not provide. And only among other women could they relax enough to discover themselves.

Dark male skins, skins like Matsushita's, shining and smooth, gleamed in the artificial spotlights of the jungle paradise. All were devoid of hair, of the hint of a blemish. Without shame they flaunted their beauty. Men in groups stood shoulder to shoulder in tiny tepid baths, comforted by the touch of flesh like their own.

Still she waited at the top of the stairs. She tried to arrange her three little towels strategically so that no unseemly flesh would be visible. Paul stood at the foot of the stairway, firm, impatient. He was the only other foreigner here; she had to join him. But it seemed inconceivable that he should see her naked, the fastidious Paul who so admired firm, flat brown skin and of another gender. Would he be repelled by sagging breasts, a belly which had always been plump, thighs which had always been full? Hadn't Matsushita felt exactly this way?

But there Paul remained, fixed, going nowhere. Slowly, gingerly, she came down the stairs, twisting and pulling at the three towels as if to make them grow larger in a vain effort to cover herself. Could he see anything? He greeted her as naturally as ever. Safe, welcoming, and all *karui*, he pretended not to notice that she was naked.

Then a problem arose: how was she to enter any of the baths without exposing herself? what to do about the moment just before she would be concealed by the waters? If she held the towels against her too long, they would become soaking wet and utterly useless, and how could she then pick them up when she had to abandon this bath and move on to the next?

The rocks were slippery. Everyone else placed their

one towel neatly on the edge of each pool and then lowered themselves into the water. If she were fast enough, she might only be exposed for an instant. This was her only hope.

They selected a nice round pool, not too hot and surrounded by pink and green tinted boulders. She lumbered up onto the edge, placing first one foot and then the other on the slick wet rocks, balancing herself as if on a tightrope, clutching the towels around her, front and back. Paul was somewhere behind her. She couldn't break her concentration to find out where. One foot landed in the water, and then the first towel slipped and then the second. White, naked, flesh was everywhere.

She gave it up.

"Oh, what the hell!" she exclaimed and let the third towel fall where it would. She plunged into the pool, allowing the hot, bitter waters to overtake her. It no longer mattered that when they moved on, Paul would see her body. He had accepted her soul and its many distortions as natural; he was here to make her accept the flesh. The wet towels lay discarded on the rocks. She moved along the paths of Ibusuki in all her nakedness, her friend, all *karui*, beside her, and she was not ashamed.

In the hottest of the pools, their arms around each other while sulfur steamed about them, they agreed without saying so that this would be the last time they would ever speak of Matsushita. But before they could attack that subject, which had once seemed so inexhaustible, they were joined by three smiling men delighted with the bonus of partaking of the healing waters in the proximity of a naked, foreign, female body. Tightly packed together, three Japanese men, one foreign male, and one foreign female breathed sulfur silently in contentment. Then she alighted, sans towels, with all the inherent danger of exposure. But the men, young peasant husbands, were so subtle that she couldn't even catch them averting their eyes as her naked white flesh overwhelmed their vision.

They found a kidney-shaped pool all to themselves.

"It has taken much too long."

"I was waiting for the right moment."

"I cannot imagine Matsushita here."

"How harassed he would be by the vulgarity of these plump bodies."

"He would never come here with you."

"It's a pity. How I would have loved to be here with him."

Their sentences remained short, staccato, washed clean.

"It's what you would have wanted, never he."

Matsushita would hereafter be "he."

Paul spoke of a lover whom he had met at these baths, a local boy. To that relation he had also brought *karui*—the cool and the dispassionate. Should his lover not appear this time, Paul would be sorry, but no more. So armed he had learned to create himself in Japan, and she must begin. It was Matsushita's loss that he was barred from such voyages of discovery.

Outside the big bay window of the greenhouse the sandy beach was deserted on this cloudy, windy, humid day. Up to their necks in sulfur, they felt the freshness of their friendship, from which jealousy, dependency, possessiveness, and need originating in the long ago and perversely rooted in the present like a ghastly mutation were all barred. They had each other, the balm of sympathy and permanent concern as soothing as the hot springs themselves. They heard the shrieks of the birds of Ibusuki, the bright green and red parrots flying through the gardens wild and free. They glimpsed the possibilities of euphoria.

Was Paul growing bored? Had he already granted her the appointed allotment of his attention? Was he already looking toward Tokyo? Did he wish to visit the baths alone that he might fill his nights with more felicitous acquaintances?

This, too, she gave up. They stood in the circle of their affection. But their friendship was not to be a foxhole. As she had let the towels slip, so she must stumble on alone. Paul would pursue those dangerous alliances of the flesh unsullied by words, which for him were life itself.

They walked on the deserted beach of Kagoshima Bay, twin souls in identical kimonos. The sun hung hazily luminous over the scarlet bougainvilleas of Ibusuki. The birds screeched.

"Have you heard about Tani?" Paul asked, with that edge to his voice which meant there was much to tell. Tani was a soft, affable director in his forties. Having won scholarships to America for documentary filmmaking he was highly Westernized, his English perfect, his winning manner making him the darling of foreign critics. His reputation was based on a humane and, rare for Japanese cinema, psychologically penetrating approach to Japan's disturbed, outcast, and lonely—children, women, peripheral people. He had long been married to a warm, vibrant actress who had played in several of his films.

"First he left Machiko for her sister, Hiroko. Then he took up with the third sister, Fumiko, the youngest, whom he's just married."

Paul was daring her to indulge in the obvious, the

forbidden, to pass moral judgment. Harmony decreed that she comply.

"He looks so good, like such an innocent." Tani, Matsushita's spiritual brother. Paul could never have liked Tani so well as when he joined the ranks of the perverse.

"None of us is innocent."

What was so special about Tani that two women, sisters, should betray each other, and a third, for the privilege of his presence? But she allowed Paul his triumph, this lesson of the master. How he enjoyed presiding over his witch's caldron, the bubbling up of the irrational, the uncontrollable which paralyzes the earnest and renders the malevolent blameless.

Nothing could insulate anyone forever from the vagaries of the human heart.

One of Paul's favorite quotations came from Colette: "To exaggerate the sorrows of love is tantamount to an indiscretion . . . it reveals the lack of that precious faculty, a sense of the ridiculous." Paul wouldn't say *she* was ridiculous. She saw it herself, accepted it, as she had accepted that he should see her naked, uncovered, unprotected.

She saw herself the fool, trailing after Matsushita, supposing all sensuality to reside in him. And now he seemed grotesque, a diminutive figure too small to be a man, wrapped tight in that satin brown skin, oblivious to the absurdity of his refined style of evasion. Nor did he care how wasteful were the bitter drops of indifference he meted out so painstakingly and with such cruelty. Matsushita became pathetic, ignorant that without her he would never have located so felicitous an opportunity to know himself, for no Japanese woman would have demanded that he offer what he would not.

No, she alone had to open up the spacious, most un-

Japanese rooms in which Matsushita could embroider undisturbed the neat flowers of his sadism. Or was he simply playing the game *she* had devised, patiently waiting for her disease to lose its grip?

One thing she knew: he would never have to explain what drove him off, or whether he had ever meant to keep all the promises he made to Paul. She would never know whether all those coy confidences he directed toward Paul were meant in fact as overtures to Paul himself. The homoeroticism of those countries where the double standard was observed so meticulously, and Japan the first of them all! It may have been that she was no more than a foil, and Matsushita hoped that the subtle Paul would understand that it was he whom Matsushita had desired all along.

But the responsibility was hers. She had been a diligent collaborator in Matsushita's cruelty, giving it shape, direction, life and breath. She was the midwife who had brought it into being. And more. She then nurtured and watched it grow, perversely satisfied as it blossomed from careless indifference to full-blown contempt, until Matsushita, ever conscious of the harmonies, could appropriately conclude their final meeting with one more lie. *"You will, you will,"* he had promised. *"Wait, Wait!"*

In these jungle baths, soothed by the healing presence of a friend who had waited through it all, she stood condemned and forgiven, the source of her own suffering. For who was Matsushita, but a small, puny man, two inches shorter than she and one whose chest was as narrow as that of a ten-year-old boy. Ludicrously antiseptic, a man without scent, dangerously effeminate, and with his hair permanent waved, a person utterly incapable of the warm, all-pervasive affection of the heterosexual male—or even of the androgynous man who finds delight in both sexes—Matsushita crawled past her in his odd dance of

deceit. And willfully, unnecessarily, she had wrapped herself crudely in the mantle of pain which he had improvised
day by day.

"I must leave in the morning," Paul said. He had not
said "we."

"I think I'll stay for a while longer," she surprised
herself by replying, and Paul nodded as if he had expected
this all along.

He knocked on her door after dinner, bearing her
going-away present, a century-old statue of the Chinese
god Hotei, who had voyaged to the southernmost tip of
Japan, burning his bridges and submitting forever to this
claustrophobic culture.

Remaining here, Paul had become one with Matsushita, his sensual kindred spirit, both of them sometimes
friendly, but no less demons of this place. Paul, too, was
locked in the calculated self-absorption of this terrain. But
for her he had paused to voice the possibility of accepting
and then reinventing oneself. She would always be grateful to him.

The next day, in the echo chamber of her memory
she could hear Koshima on that afternoon in Kyoto three
years before, demanding an account of her motives for
studying Japan and the Japanese. Like her, he too struggled against paralyzing tradition, refusing to accept the
seductive mask of the exotic, forcing sunlight in upon the
ancient, rotting crannies of this culture. It was Koshima
who battled to be free of the feudalism of the past, Matsushita who dwelt among dusty hierarchies which whispered that he could say and do what he would to a woman
and a foreigner and the powers of darkness would not de-
scend upon him. Yet Koshima had been wrong to accuse
her of being unable to love anything Japanese. Surely she

had loved Matsushita, his delicacy, his infinite capacity to communicate by gesture, without words, the venerable texture of his beauty. She had loved him as much as she had ever loved anyone.

In the magnificence of Japanese nature she had been returned to herself and so she loved Japan too. In the waters of Ibusuki she had learned to face a ravaging disease of the psyche and to hold it in check.

Was she immune at last? It was too soon to tell. Washed clean in the healing waters of Ibusuki, she had taken a step toward herself.

But who could tell if tomorrow she might not follow another Matsushita down the winding alleys of some decaying city, feverishly in pursuit of an equally obscure and exquisite object?

As she walked along the beach that afternoon, a deeper truth rose up, catching her unawares. And she knew now, beyond doubt, that it had not been Matsushita at the airport on the day of her return to Japan. It could not have been Matsushita at all! Matsushita would have worn the white Cardin jumpsuit, the orange silk shirt, the coy little-boy grin. The man she saw had been no more than a slight look-alike, a phantom, the image of her enslavement, her desire. No, it was not Matsushita.

Like the samisen-player–rapist of Paul's story, Matsushita had forced what she said she wanted down her throat. Her obsession had justified his anger. Wasn't his violence the only logical reaction of a man who was loved not for himself, as he was, but for what she was bent on making of him?

She had never loved Matsushita at all! And indeed how could she? She never really knew him, never learned all that much about him. She had wanted something from him which could have been demanded of anyone. No wonder then that when Matsushita finally called her to him, she still hadn't been satisfied; she still hadn't attained her heart's desire. She had demanded that he play a part in a fantasy, and he had rejected the script as having nothing to do with him. For she had wanted of Matsushita only what she could make of him, as a dangerously possessive mother denies the reality of her child in pursuit of what she would have him be for her.

Matsushita was not the bad father whose love she could hope to win one day against all odds, becoming at the last a fountain of love, protection, solace, and escape. She had staked all in the mythology of this quest and so denied them both their separate realities.

And what of those demons which ceaselessly sent her to men dedicated to forgetting that they had ever known her? Could they be forever banished, chained up here in Ibusuki, in Kagoshima, where they could never get at her again?

She saw them for the rest of her life at her heels. They might overtake her again. But Paul had taught her all he knew, the only lasting defense against these monstrous creatures spawned and nurtured throughout her childhood with enough flesh on them to last a lifetime. They were always with her, but she was also herself looking out at them as they regrouped, strategized, and rose in pursuit with a thunderous shuddering of wings. She knew she could live apart from what they had the power to make her do. She could turn bright, glaring spotlights on them at any time, klieg lights, blinding lights which would blind them and blind her and make them equal adversaries once more. She could send them, if not forever, never forever, on their way. They would always be nipping at her heels, but she could still live.